MEMORIES
OF THE
BLUE EYES
AN ANTHOLOGY OF SHORT STORIES

PETER AMALRAJAN

Copyright © 2017 Peter Amalrajan

ISBN: 978-0-244-03580-8

All rights reserved, including the right to reproduce this book, or portions thereof in any form. No part of this text may be reproduced, transmitted, downloaded, decompiled, reverse engineered, or stored, in any form or introduced into any information storage and retrieval system, in any form or by any means, whether electronic or mechanical without the express written permission of the author.

To everyone who has made a difference.
You know who you are.

Disclaimer: The characters in the stories are completely fictional. Any resemblance to any real people or incidents are truly coincidental – mainly because, the author is not hugely knowledgeable. Even if there was such person or story in life, he just would not know!

*A black Chevy and
a white dress*

Part I: The Black Chevrolet Camaro

His line manager quoted once, *'I won't call you a workaholic because that word does not serve justice. Work is more than an addiction to you.'*

That line pretty much summarised what he had done in the last few years. First in, last out – he was very seriously addicted to work. No party, no rest, well, almost no life outside of work. Neither anyone knew how he was before nor did he show any signs of that other life.

Out of the blue on a bright day, he called in late to the office. When he walked into the office a couple of hours later than usual, his face was unusually lit with a bright smile – a sign of accomplishment. And, when he was about to leave for the day in the evening - that too before anyone else, everyone's curiosity was kindled.

'Looks like someone's finally got a life', giggled the bespectacled lady in the third cabin from his.

He wished the security guard a good evening and jogged – well, almost ran to the parking lot. He felt like he had just been unnerved by a few shots of Sambuca.

If someone had stopped him on the way, to quench their curiosity, then they would have come to know about the secret - the secret behind his sudden burst of enthusiasm. If they had followed him along to the parking lot, they would have met **her** - the beauty who he had fallen head over heels for, with an unknown measure of awe.

He stood for a second and looked at her face to face. She was stunning in black – a gorgeous sight! No wonder he had fallen in love with her at first sight – who wouldn't?

She stood a few feet away from him - his new-found love. If she had been human, Cleopatra would have been the reference for comparison. Since she was a car, there were no words in stock. His very own Chevrolet Camaro in royal black. Her beauty and radiance would have beaten Cleopatra hands down. And, the love he had for his Chevrolet Camaro was a lot more than what Antony had for Cleopatra.

He had booked his Chevy Camaro a long time ago and had been eagerly waiting like a child. His was the first to be delivered by the dealer. He had seen a real Chevy Camaro only once before other than the one from the Transformers movies. And, that car he had seen was a Camaro in white. His Chevy Camaro, in black, was beyond any means, a stunner of a car. The moment he touched the car for the first time, he knew that the Chevy was going to be more than just a car.

The interior of a Chevrolet Camaro was the very definition of 'State of the art'. The authentic leather, the temperature control to the last degree, the comfort on the sexy steering wheel, the stylish gears that slid with ease, the BOSE surround sound system, the latest GPS for a pin point location, the anti-theft fingerprint scanners, the much talked about voice recognition – you could just go on and on and on. He wished his journey would never end every time he got into his Chevy Camaro.

He loved driving his Chevy. He was tempted many a time to just stand on top of his Camaro with his arms wide open and shout 'I'm the king of the world' – just like Leo did in Titanic. He didn't like it when someone referred to his car as 'it'. He would correct them to say 'her'. That was how he treated it, sorry, treated her - the love of his life, his black Chevrolet Camaro.

He was sometimes asked if anything or anyone – a real person for that matter, had come so close to his life lately. That was a simple question with a very simple 'No' as the answer. If the question was a little farfetched, changing the 'lately' to 'ever', then that would have turned into a slightly more complicated question.

If the question had been *'had anyone come close to his life ever before?'*, then his answer would have been a thoughtful 'yes'.

Yes, there had been someone in the past - the past which stayed almost forgotten, the past which he wanted to stay forgotten.

There was a girl who he had been deeply in love with. She was a lovely girl with bright blue eyes, beautiful curly hair and a fairy tale name. She loved white, the serene color of peace. Gorgeous as she was adorable. Smart as she was sweet. She was William Shakespeare's Portia, George Eliot's Eppie, Jane Austen's Lizzy and – the list would be never ending. Every other great literary work seemed to have a beautiful leading lady just like her. It was love at first sight then too and a poetic one nevertheless.

It was a rainy day. She was dressed in white and was waiting at a bus stop with a bright red umbrella. She was playing like a little child with the water dazzling on the glass. Along he came cursing the rain till that moment. When he saw her, he realised that the rain was a blessing in disguise. The Mini Cooper that he owned back then came to a slow stop near her. He saved her from the storm and dropped her home. He didn't even take her name but she took his heart along.

After a series of deliberately accidental meetings, things took a positive turn. She reciprocated his love after almost a year. After that years vanished like minutes. They took life as it came with unending episodes of happiness. Even their arguments were sweet and romantic. Their story of love would have captured a place among the greats of Allie - Noah, Anna - William and Jessie - Karthik. And, things went towards a 'happily ever after' fairy tale ending. All was well until that fateful day.

He was the one who always drove – no matter where and no matter when. But that day was different. They had had an argument in the morning. There was an awkward silence for over an hour and then she drove away in his car – probably to the church where she usually went to calm down. But, little did he know that she was never going to come back to him – not alive at least. It had snowed the previous night and a truck on the opposite lane had lost control, slid across the signal and rammed into the driver's side of the Mini. She came back in a coffin, dressed in beautiful white.

For over a year, he kept punishing himself for whatever had happened. If he had not argued with her, if he had not let her drive alone, if he had not waited but apologised. Only if... There were a lot of things that he could have done. But, he hadn't and she had left him forever taking with her all the happiness she had given him.

The days that followed her demise were inexplicable. He could not comprehend her death and believed that she was alive. Sometimes she smiled at him when he drove past bus stops.

Sometimes she whispered in his ears when he was asleep. He saw her in the church, he saw her in the garden, he saw her in almost every place they had spent their time together.

The thought that he could have done a lot to have avoided the tragedy and the thought that he was not able to save his girl was sculpted into his mind. He was slowly going insane and he had turned to drugs and alcohol as a remedy.

It took him three long years to get over the addiction. And it took even more time to rehabilitate and get to where he had gotten now. He did not want to go back to his past. He just wanted it to stay forgotten, for his own good. He was a new man now and just as he had gotten a grip over his life, he had fallen in love with his Chevy Camaro.

He loved his time driving to the office every morning. He loved his time driving home every evening. He loved the time he drove to anywhere at all. He even loved the time he waited in his Chevy for the traffic lights to turn green. This love story was beyond words too.

Part II: The rainy night

He was working late on that rainy August day. It was close to eight but the sun had just begun to set and it was pretty bright. A beautiful rainbow had formed fully on the eastern sky – it looked very beautiful indeed.

'It's time to wrap up for the day', insisted his colleague and he obliged. He jumped into his Camaro who roared to life and they were on their way home.

The glittering road, the splashing water and the extra drift at the sharp corners, he loved it more than ever. He had an absolute control over his driving. His Camaro did as he told her to - Stop where he wanted her to stop, turn where he wanted her to turn, drift to the exact position where he wanted her to drift to. If the drift had to be six and a half feet, his Chevy would do exactly that. Nothing more, nothing less. Even in the most drastic conditions his driving was perfect to the 'T'.

The sun had almost set with its golden rays turning to a beautiful orange. It would have been a few minutes since he had started and he came towards a deserted signal just before the motorway. As he inched closer to the signal, the lights turned green. It brought a smile to his lips. He drove faster and was about a few hundred metres away from the last of the bus stops on the road. As he came closer, he saw a lonely figure waiting at the bus stop.

He took his foot off of the gas pedal and his Chevy slowed down. The image of the person standing in the bus stop slowly became clear in the rain. It was a girl in a white dress standing with a red umbrella. A lot of memories crossed his mind but he had learnt enough to brush them away. He stopped his Chevy Camaro close to the bus stop. He lowered the glass of the passenger window just enough to talk to the girl.

The girl appeared to be totally drenched in the rain. Her skin was pale obviously due to the chillness. Her eyes were half closed as if she was going to fall asleep in the next few minutes. She wore no jewels but looked radiant. The fingers holding the umbrella were slightly trembling. She had a weird but beautiful dragon tattoo on her shoulder which crept up to the middle of her neck.

He waited for a couple of seconds for her to lift her face up to see him. But she stood there as if she didn't even know that he was there.

'Excuse me?', he said in a normal tone. She did not react which made him think that he was not loud enough.

'Excuse me?', he said in a louder voice hoping she would hear. But, the response remained the same.

The next moment a bright lighting struck in the direction behind him. For a second it was so bright like standing in the sun at noon. The thunder that followed a few seconds later was so loud that he could feel the ground below him shake for a second. Those few seconds were really frightening. But against all odds, the girl did not even wince.

'What on earth is wrong with her?', he whispered to himself.

As he prepared himself to ask the girl if she wanted a ride home, he noticed in the rear-view mirror that a bus was approaching from far behind. He hesitated for a second and decided that it would be better for him to leave the girl in peace. After all she was in the bus stop and the bus would be there in the next few seconds.

He shifted into gear and moved away. He kept checking the mirror. As he took the left turn to the motorway, he saw that the bus had reached the bus stop but the girl was not to be seen anywhere.

For the next couple of miles, his thoughts kept going back to the girl he saw in the bus stop. He felt nervous about the similarities of the events in the past - The bus stop on a rainy day, the girl in a white dress and the red umbrella. He could not keep the girl who he had loved out of his mind. However much he tried, her memories kept coming back again and again. His nightmares were returning, he thought. He went into a quasi-stable state as if he was hypnotised.

A sudden loud horn brought his wavering thoughts back to reality. The first thing he noticed was a pair of bright lights approaching him at a fast pace. He got back to his senses just in time to steer his Chevy out of the way of the bright lights which belonged to a 20 tonne truck. Just as the truck went past he realised how far he had gone into the opposite lane.

He took a deep breath to control his nervousness and continued his drive up the motorway. He had to forget everything and focus on his driving. At the current speed and being on the deserted motorway, he would reach home in the next forty minutes. He took a few slow but steady breaths and gripped the steering wheel harder to get things under control. And then, it happened.

He approached a roundabout, the last one for the day. After that roundabout, it was going to be just a straight road up hill. He would have to take the second exit. He crossed the first exit and with the usual ease reached the second. Just as he was going to straighten his steering wheel to guide his Chevy into the second exit, the steering wheel resisted to turn. The car just kept taking the curve. He pulled the steering wheel hard but it did not budge for the next few seconds. Not until they were closer to the third and final exit.

Just as the Chevy reached the third exit, steering wheel came to life and he guided his car into the exit and onto the main road. As he sped away into the road he had not much used in the past, he was trying to comprehend what just happened. How did it happen? How and why did the steering wheel act as if it was locked on the curve?

He slowed down and came to a halt on the hard shoulder on the left. He just sat there for a few minutes wondering if everything was alright. He turned the steering wheel all the way in both the directions. There was not even a slight hinge in the movement. It was as perfect and smooth as ever.

'What has gotten into you?', he asked his Chevy. Or, was he imagining something?

He stepped on the gas a minute later and was off in the direction which was totally new to him. He had to get around to the other side of the road somehow, go all the way back to the roundabout and take the usual motorway. He hoped he would get a chance to turn around at the earliest.

He drove on. Traffic was nonexistent and there were no speed cameras in sight. He gave it all to his Chevy Camaro and she roared to life like a lioness chasing her prey. The speed hit 115 mph. Still, he could not see any speed cameras, traffic or an opportunity to turn around to the opposite lanes.

Finally, a traffic signal appeared in sight at around two hundred meters dead straight ahead.

'Time to slow down', he told himself.

He took his foot off the gas pedal and waited for a second. Something was strange – very strange. The digital speed dial still read 115 mph. After a couple of seconds it was still on 115 mph. The car was closer to the traffic signal now. He could see at least four more cars waiting at the signal.

After four seconds, the speed was no more 115 mph - it read 117 mph. And a second later it was 119 mph. The speed was fast increasing.

Blood drained from his face. His heart was beating at the rate of 120 beats per minute. The veins in his hands were pumped up and about to burst through his skin. His grip on the steering wheel was so immense that he could feel it crumble under his grip. His eyes had turned red under pressure.

He slammed the brake pedal all the way down to the floor of the car. He slammed it again and again but there was not even a slightest sign of the car slowing down. It was still gaining speed. 125 mph read the dial and still gaining. He tried his last resort, the hand brake - without even giving a thought about what could happen at that speed. But, it appeared to be jammed and he was not able to pull it up.

The signal was just within reach and the cars waiting for the signals were just a few yards away. He was definitely going to crash into the cars in front. He knew that it was going to be the end of it. At the speed he was travelling, survival was not even a question. He lost hope and closed his eyes.

He shouted at the top of his voice *'OH GOD!!!'*

When someone knew that their time was fast approaching, and all they had to do was just wait for it, minutes were like years. For him, those few seconds were like millenniums. He waited and waited for his beautiful black Chevy Camaro to crash into the car in front and to take him along with her forever. He waited and waited. But the moment never came. He slowly opened his eyes.

His Chevy Camaro stood at a safe distance away from the car in front. It was still red at the signal. He did not know how and he did not know why. For some reason beyond reasoning, the car had kept gaining speed and had come to a stop by itself. Maybe he was hallucinating? Was there another plausible reason to this at all?

Whatever it was, he was not dead, not yet. But there was a big question about what was happening and whether he would make it home safely. And, he knew the answer. There was no way he would be able to drive safely. If there was something wrong with him or if he was for some reason hallucinating, then he could cause harm to others by driving his beloved Camaro.

It was high time he got out of the car, he decided. He pulled the handle to open the door. It wouldn't open. He pulled it again hard but still no luck.

'Oh God, not again', he thought. Just when he was going to freak out, he realised a simple mistake. He had not tapped open the lock before fighting with the door handle. He could not help but smile.

Just as he was going to open the door, a Vauxhall Insignia came up to the signal and stopped very close to his Chevy. He pulled the door handle but could only open the door to about half a foot and it was already touching the Insignia that had just arrived. There was no way he would be able to get out now. And, the signal turned green.

He thought he would just wait for the cars to move while he can figure something out. The lane in which he was waiting began to clear very fast. He didn't want to move. He was scared to move forward. Then there was a loud horn from behind. A huge vehicle, he could not identify what it was, was fast approaching. And, to make it worse, it was not slowing down. Another LOUD horn made him shiver even more.

He had no choice; he had to drive out of the way and fast. He throttled out of the way into the road ahead. He kept driving for the next eight to ten minutes hoping he would find a way out of there. And then he realised that he was alone again. The road had turned completely dark. It looked like he and his Chevy were the only ones on the entire stretch of the road.

He did not know where all those cars in the traffic signal had gone. He checked his rearview mirror. The huge vehicle that was driving at him in full speed was out of sight too.

'Damn the cars and Damn this road!', he cursed.

A lightning and thunder struck eight seconds apart as if declaring that the storm was near. It started raining once again. He had driven many times in the rain and snow, once through a hail but there was something different in the way it was raining.

'Damn the rain too!', he sighed.

The windshield wipers were doing their best but with the speed at which the rain was pouring, there was not much they could do to clear the view. The temperature in the car was optimum that the rain did not cause the usual haze on the inside. Things were manageable.

That was what he thought till the lights showed something unrecognisable. He was not able to see beyond it and it was almost in the nick of the moment when he realised that it was a truck parked in the middle of the road without any kind of indicators switched on.

He rammed the brakes but there was not even a slight sign of slowing down. He tried pulling the handbrake but they would not budge.

'Holy mother, it's happening again', he cried out. His heart was beating faster and his eyes were unable to adjust to the pressure.

'Oh God, NOOOO!!!', he shouted. And, at the last minute, the steering wheel turned quickly by itself and the hand brake engaged without him even touching it. The wheel kept steering all the way to the left. And the Chevy drifted like a speedboat and avoided the truck by a little more than an inch.

He continued screaming till his lungs were out of air. The intracranial pressure was immense. There was a loud banging inside his head. He could feel the blood dripping down his nose. His heart was beating at a pace beyond count.

'Oh God, please!!', he cried. Tears rained down his face. It was the first time he had cried in a long time.

His beloved Chevrolet Camaro stood by the side of the truck for a while. He was unable to even lift his hands up to the steering wheel. He was in a state of pure shock. He was shivering like a cymbal struck at the end of an opera. It was as if he had woken up in an unrecognisable vacuum far deep in the galaxy.

The car shifted into gear moved ahead all by itself. Everything was blurred beyond imagination. It was pitch black and all he could see was the road which the lights showed. The intensity of the blur was slowly increasing along with the speed of the car. Then the lights went out and it was total darkness. And then, he blacked out.

When he woke up, it was difficult for him to understand where was. His eyes adjusted to the situation. It was still dark and it was still drizzling. He looked at his watch which read 23:43. He could see a sign board up ahead but it was too dark for him to read. He switched on the ignition and turned on the lights. The sign board said the name of a village.

The name of the village sounded familiar but he did not know why. He could not remember how he had gotten there. He closed his eyes to calm down and think. The harder he thought about it the more difficult it was for him to understand. Then it struck him like a bolt - the chain of events that had occurred earlier. A chill went down his spine.

He opened the door and jumped out of the car. He did not know how and why his Chevy had not responded to his maneuvers. The car had driven all on its own. He did not know for how long and how far but his car had not been under his control. It was possessed by something beyond his power of reasoning.

He stood out of his car and looked at it. It looked as gorgeous as ever. There was not even a tiny scratch anywhere - even after all that had happened. But he knew something was not right. There was something that he had learnt the hard way. The line between the good and the evil, elixir and poison, beauty and the beast was just a blur and you would never know when one form took over the other.

He did not know if the black Chevy standing in front of him was still the beauty he fell in love with or some unknown beast that had taken control. He did not know and maybe he never will. He slowly took a few steps away from the car. It was pitch black all around. He did not know which way to go. He looked at the sign board again. Then it struck him.

He had taken this road a long time ago, many years ago. He had met her here for the first time, the girl he had fallen in love with. The bus stop was probably half a mile away, where he had met that lovely girl on that lovely rainy day. But what he could not understand was why he had been brought here? The reason behind all that happened over the last few hours was non-existent.

He looked at his mobile phone. There was no signal. He tried calling the emergency numbers but there was no sound whatsoever. The line remained silent.

The drizzling had stopped and a dense fog had set in. The silence was intense without even a speck of a noise. His eyes searched for a while trying to find something somewhere in the dark. A lightning in a far distance showed him the way. In those few seconds of the bright light, he saw a footpath going steep down from the road and there was a cabin in the far end. And he could see a feeble light through the window.

Part III: The Cabin

He walked swiftly towards the cabin hoping he could get some help. Another lightning struck lighting up the path in front of him. The path looked vacant and there were no obstacles till the cabin. He reached the door and waited. Did he really have to disturb someone at this time in the night? Did he have any other option?

He hesitated but knew he had to get help. He pressed the doorbell. He was sure he heard a ring of the bell on the inside. He pressed the bell again with his ears close to the door. The bell did ring but there seemed to be no life on the other side of the door.

'Hello...?', he shouted. He banged the door a couple of times.

'Hello...? Anybody home...?', he shouted again banging the door another couple of times.

'Hello...?', he shouted again – trying to be clear and loud amidst the never-ending perspiration and palpitation.

He waited for what felt like an era hoping someone would open the door. But no one did. The hope he had about receiving some help from here was fast going down. No one was going to come out.

Just as he turned around, a voice in him said, *'the door is open'* and as if commanded by someone he touched the doorknob. To his surprise, the door opened without even a hint of resistance. For a second it was relief and the next second it was fear that struck him.

A cabin in the middle of nowhere and the door was open. Something was far from being alright. Was this some kind of a trap that he was stepping into? Did someone want him here at this exact time? He gathered some courage and took a step into the cabin.

'Is anyone there?', he shouted, taking one step at a time into the cabin.

'Hello... Is anyone th...?', he didn't even finish the sentence when he saw the condition of the room he stepped into. The room was in total disarray. Everything, every single thing, was shattered or upside down - as if the place had been ransacked.

He sensed trouble and decided to get out of the place. Just as he was about to take a step out of the room, he noticed something on the floor at the far end of the room. He wished he had not seen it.

BLOOD! There were streaks and streaks of blood stretching from the far end of this room into the next. Someone or something had been dragged on the floor. He took a few steps forward careful not to disturb anything in the room. As he came closer, he was sure it was blood. It had not dried up fully so whatever had happened in this room had happened not very long ago.

He followed the blood strains slowly and carefully. His heart was filled with fear and his mind was wishing that this was just a dream. When his eyes reached the end of the trail of blood, his head went into a violent spin, his knees buckled and his bowels rolled over. What he saw would have had this effect on even the most hard-hearted. He almost threw up.

It took him a few minutes to cope up with the situation but he was unable to get a complete hold of himself. He raised his eyes to look at the scene again. What he saw was a scene out of a slasher flick.

A girl had been badly beaten with blood dripping from every inch of her body and was hung by a rope tied to the ceiling. Her jaw was broken and her face was almost out of shape. One of her eyes was swollen so badly and her face was unrecognizable. She had been stabbed multiple times on her arms, abdomen and thighs. Her ankle was broken and so were a few of her toes. There were no visible stab wounds to her chest and neck.

Just as his eyes grazed her neck, he noticed the weird but beautiful dragon tattoo on her neck. He had seen it earlier that night. It was the girl in the bus stop, the girl who showed no visible reaction when he had offered her a drive home. That girl in a white dress - Someone had killed her.

Who was she?!

Why would someone kill her?!

If the motive was to kill the girl with a knife, why not slice her throat or stab her heart? He had no answer to this but looking at all the blood, looked like whoever did this wanted to bleed her to death. It was an execution more than just a murder.

His teeth were chattering in fear. He could not control his heavy breathing. He tried to clear his mind; he had to get out of there. He had already had an inexplicable night and amidst all that he did not want to be there, not in a cabin where a girl had been executed. He had to get away from there.

Just as he was about to take a step away, he heard a very mild cough. His heart skipped a beat – someone else was in the house.

He turned around with his eyes wildly searching for whoever it was. All he could see was the dead girl. There was no one else. Given the chain of events, it was more probable that he had imagined it.

His search came to an end with his eyes fixed on the face of the girl. He remembered how beautiful she looked when he had seen her earlier. How could someone show this kind of a cruelty to another human being? As he kept looking at her, tears started flowing down his eyes. He did not even realize that he was crying.

And then, the girl took a deep breath. He was taken aback and fell on his back pushed by a sudden rush of fear. And then, there was an intense silence. His thoughts were blurred and he did not know if she had really taken a breath. He did not dare to get up but he kept looking at the girl with his eyes wide open. He waited and waited and waited.

She took another deep breath.

'Bloody hell, she is alive!!!', he freaked.

'Oh, my god she is alive!!!', he shrieked again.

He knew he had a very meagre chance of helping the girl – to help her get back from what looked like the brink of death.

His mind was racing. Driving at the moment was not a good idea. He did not know where he was except for the sign board. He did not even remember how he had gotten here years ago. His mobile was out of signal and not even the emergency numbers were working. He closed his eyes and tried to concentrate. It was immensely impossible but he had to do something. He tried again and he remembered.

Amidst the scattered and battered stuff in the first room of the cabin he had seen a cordless phone. He ran to the other room with his eyes yearning for the sight of the phone. He found it on a broken flower vase. He grabbed it hoping it was still working.

He pressed '9... 9... 9...' and pressed call. It was silent for a full ten seconds. And then it rang on the other end. After what sounded like an era, there was an answer.

'Emergency services, how can we be of assistance?', he breathed a huge sigh of relief.

All he could give them was the sign board which said the name of the village and the cabin along the footpath. He did not know if the girl had much time left. He did not know if emergency services would come in time to save her. He did not know – in the same way as he did not know who she was or how he had gotten there in the middle of a dark stormy night.

Help finally came in. The police took control of the scene and the girl was taken out of the place in a chopper. Her condition was termed as Critical, though he had a strong feeling that she would make it. He was questioned by the detectives on who he was and how he had found her. He explained how his Chevy had a break down – almost the same nervous breakdown as he had had, he told himself. He had seen the cabin out there and tried to get some help.

His story was a bit naïve but the fingerprints in the cabin, on the first look, did not match his except for the one on the phone. Though the police, in theory, had his name on the list of suspects because he was the first to call, there was little doubt in anyone's mind. He was asked to take a cab home and respond back if there were any questions for him.

His beautiful Chevy was towed away just as the cab came to the scene. It was around 06:00 in the morning when he got into the cab. He sat in the backseat with his eyes closed listening to the radio. The morning show on the radio had just gone into the second segment *'Beyond the power of human reasoning'*.

The Asian lady presenting the show was explaining something which he was not even paying a grain of attention. Something she said caused a stir in his thoughts and the next moment his complete attention was on what the lady was saying.

'The Japanese people have a strong belief in souls searching for help, especially in the last few moments before parting ways with the human body. The cry for help is louder when death knocks at the door in horrible ways. During this time, the power of the soul is so immense that they reach out to the living world - to ask for help.'

'It's been impossible to prove this but there are a lot of real life accounts backing this. In late 1987, an old farmer from Marahito had walked a long distance guided by an unknown force to save a young man who had been in a horrible road accident. Around Christmas time in the year 1996, a lady from the outskirts of Tokyo who was brutally hurt by an intruder was saved by an unknown man. The man had seen the same lady crying for help while he was driving in a deserted road almost ten miles away. And more recently in the year 2009, a man had saved a kidnapped child who was left to suffocate in a closed bin. The man had said that his car had gone violently out of

control and had driven down the slope to the backyard where he had found the child.'

'There are a lot of accounts similar to these not only in Japan but around the world. Though there is no scientific proof, people in Japan believe strongly in this', and the voice on the radio faded as he drifted slowly into his own world.

He still had his eyes closed. He was still trying to comprehend. No one was going to believe this. Even he himself had trouble believing it. But he had to accept it. On a rainy night, he had had an inexplicable and bizarre encounter with the soul of a dying girl – ***the girl in a white dress***

Just because...

As my eyes begin to close and my vision goes dark, I think of the happy moments of my life. They seem like far and distant memories. But the little memories of my little family; my mom and my dad are bright.

I am down on the ground and I try to see through the blur. I can see a few people running towards me but I do not want to find out if they are going to inflict more pain or if they are coming to help. I have no energy to wait for them. I decide to finally give up. There is nothing more for me to even decide. I give up.

My story so far...

I didn't know my parents. As far as I knew, I was picked up from a garbage dump on the outskirts of an unknown Indian city. Someone somewhere wanted to keep me alive. Their generosity stopped there, though. They put me in an orphanage. We little ones there liked to call it an "Orphanage". But it was more a huge shed-like shelter for orphans like us.

There was never enough food for us, never enough space to sleep, never enough anything. I was too little to remember the horrible things that happened there. But even then, there were a few things that could never be erased from my mind. The tears of the new orphans who were put into the confined space with us, the moaning of the ones that missed their families, the tears of joy when there was food available for all of us. There were a never-ending pangs of sadness etched into our lives.

But once in every few weeks something would happen, a silver lining. Someone from somewhere would come to our orphanage to adopt one of us. That was a ticket to a better world and a better life. Whenever that happened, we all got good food the night before, a long and good night's sleep and more importantly we all got cleaned up - shining like new. We would all be made to stand in line the next day. Every minute standing there would be exciting. Every one of us would hope that we would be selected over the others. When we were not the lucky ones, we would be sad for only a second but we would rejoice for our little brother or sister who was destined for better life.

I would hope every time that it was my turn to live a happier life. And as every disappointment came along, I hoped more and more.

"My time would come", I told myself every night.

That was when I met George. There was no 'show' planned for him. He just walked in one morning with a calm and soothing smile. He looked at all of us and pointed his finger at me and nodded me to come to him. I was about two years old then. I was a bit hesitant at first. But I slowly walked towards him. He looked into my eyes for a good few seconds. He then gave a pat on my back and said those words every single one of my brothers and sisters there was waiting to hear.

"Let's go home, little one!"

An unknown excitement rushed through me. I did not know what to say. I could hear my mates cheering for me. As I had hoped for, my time for a better life was finally there. I gave a hesitant nod and walked along with George. I took one last look at the others and nodded them a sad goodbye. I was quite sure that their time would come too.

"You can call me George!", he said as I got into the car with him. *"What's your name?"*

I had no answer for him. I had only then realised that I had never had a name. All for two years, I had no name - what a sad life I had had till then. As if he had read my mind, he said *"Oh, don't worry. I will give you a name",* he said as we drove away.

After what looked like a good couple of hours, he announced that we were home. We waited outside for a few minutes for someone to open the door. After having been shut in the shed for a very long time, the fresh air and the brightness of the day was so refreshing. I almost wanted to lie back and just soak in the moment. And then, someone opened the door.

I had not met many people before but the person who opened the door was the most serenely beautiful person I had ever seen. Those blue eyes showed such kindness that even the unhappiest person would feel touched. No one would ever feel angry seeing such an angelic face, I thought.

"This is Anna", George said and they both took me into their home. Whatever be their names, I had at that moment decided that they were going to be my mom and dad. After two long years in a shit-hole, I knew immediately that I had a family.

Though I was adopted, both of them showered nothing but love on me. They took care of me as if I was their own. Having not spoken to anyone ever before, I was shy and embarrassed to even talk properly to them. But they brought me out of my shell and helped me to be normal with them. I had my own space, my own bed and food every time I was hungry - it was heaven to me. I didn't know about any Gods then. But George and Anna were real Gods to me. I called them mom and dad in my own language - whether they understood me or not I did not know. I loved every moment I was around them.

There was a little sadness once in a while in mom's eyes, though. She would lighten up seeing me and there would be nothing but joy in her eyes. It took me a good few months to understand what had been the reason behind it. George and Anna had been married for twelve years and the fact that she was not able to bear a child of her own was slowly chiseling away the happiness in her life.

She would pray every day asking God for a child. When I knew the story, I started praying with her. I knew I would be her elder child and I was asking God for a brother or sister. I prayed for the first time in my life for mom and dad. Every time she shed a tear, I would be by her side trying to wipe off the tears. Dad did his best to cheer her up too.

And our prayers were answered. Mom told me the news first. Even dad had to wait till that evening to hear the news. I remembered the moment very vividly for months to come. "I was going to have a brother or sister!!". When I saw the happiness in her blue eyes, I almost was moved to tears.

A few months later my brother was born - yes, he was my brother. He was too little to even know who I was. His arrival was the final piece of the happiness puzzle in our little home. There was never-ending joy at home. Mom and dad were at their happiest best. They both showed no change in the way they loved me. By that time, it was four years of nothing but pure love.

And then, fate struck. It struck hard. My parents left us with our neighbours for a few hours to meet a friend. The minute my dad started the car, I knew something was wrong. I could not explain my thoughts to him in a way he could understand. My way of telling them not to leave was only making them more annoyed. And just as they reached the signal at the end of the road, I saw the car run over by a high-speed truck crushing my parents and the lives of me and my brother.

When my parents died, there was sadness in our house for about three weeks. There were loads and loads of relatives visiting us. When the mourning period was over, the serious discussions and arguments began. There were ugly arguments over who would get what from my mom and dad's possessions. These were the relatives whom I had never seen in my entire time with mom and dad. My brother was just three years old. He did not understand a single thing that was going on. And I was just treated like an outsider. One by one, they decided who got the money, the jewels, the land my dad had owned, who would get to settle the loans and debts - all that stuff. It became clearer and clearer that my brother and I were not at all in their range of interest.

At last by some divine intervention, a distant relative decided to take my brother in. I was so happy when the decision was made. I was never part of the family in their eyes. I was just treated as adopted filth. But there was a mild hope in my mind that they would take me along with them. I just tagged along with him on the final day hoping someone would notice me as well.

Of course, they noticed me. Just as the moment came for my brother to leave with that distant relative, they noticed me trying to get into the car along with him. The old man kicked me hard that I fell quite far from the vehicle. I was shocked and scared that they were just going to leave me on the road. I was just seven years old and why they left me was something I could never understand.

I ran behind the car as fast as I could, hoping my brother would convince them to stop the car and get them to take me with them. I could see him talking to the people in the car. But as they gained distance, the hope in my heart faded away quicker than the car.

As I stood gasping for air, I just hoped my brother would turn around to see me one last time. I was hoping he would be in tears when he looked at me and said a final goodbye. But that just stayed a hope. It ripped my heart open and I cried for what seemed like an eternity. I was just left behind like garbage on the road.

What did they think I could do? I was seven years old and they left me on the street. I had a lovely home, I had mom and dad. Everything had disappeared in a flash - but why?

I went door to door to my neighbours. Some gave me food. Some gave me a bit of space outside their gates for me to stay for some time. But majority of them treated me like girdle. The rainy days were the worst and I did not know what I could do when the winter arrived. Days went by and I lived like a nomad. I gathered food from the rubbish. I looked at the other kids who used to play with me and my brother during the good days. They didn't even spare a second for me. Some didn't even recognize me. A sense of hatred slowly grew in me.

I could never understand how the world could just change in a moment!

I struggled to survive. I saw a bunch of others like me under an old bridge. They seem to have been living the same life for quite a long time. I thought my life would have been better had I not known any of the comforts in life. I found the transition unbearable. Months went by since my life turned topsy turvy and the memories of the happy days began to fade. No one recognized me anymore. An old man gave me food that day. The food had gone sour but I had to eat something to stay alive. I overheard that the festival of Diwali was fast approaching.

There were moments I dreaded in life and Diwali was one of them. The mention of Diwali sent a weird feeling down my stomach. I, at least, had a house to hide in before but I was not sure what I would do come Diwali day. I was scared of firecrackers. It sounded silly to everyone but it was the truth. I was scared to death

For a brief moment, the joys of my previous Diwali rushed through my mind the little family, the food, the happiness mainly. The memories were a bit blurred given how my life had ended up. I had some vivid memories of my mom and dad giving me a cuddle when I was scared of the very loud crackers some neighbour kids were bursting. For the first time in a long time, I missed them deeply. I missed them dearly.

I tried talking to my new friends - my vagabond friends in a half-finished construction site. Some of the elder ones laughed at me when I talked about my fears. But a few of them in the similar age group as me had some consoling words.

The couple of days before the festival were weird. Everyone was in some sort of hurry. No one really saw I was there. They were busy decorating the houses, shopping and of course the sporadic fire crackers. I envied their joy. I slowly became jealous of their happiness. But I knew that "jealous" was all I could be.

And then it got worse.

On the day before Diwali everyone went berserk. The situation went haywire. There were noises from the crackers every other second. Some were loud and some were distant. But every sound sent a shudder through me. A few of my friends laughed at me while others who were as frightened as me gave me company. The sounds became immensely intolerable. Every bang impacted my thinking. Every distant burst of noise got me a tiny bit crankier than I already was. I wanted to scream. I wanted it all to end.

I closed my eyes and tried to bury myself in the corner of a dark alley. I wished the world would go quiet right that second. But nothing happened. It kept getting worse every second. The noises became louder and they got nearer. I wished it was not true and my brain, in its tired and scared state, was just imagining things. I slowly opened my eyes.

A few little kids were playing a few feet away from me. They looked about ten years old. Then I realised the horror. They were playing with fire crackers. Every sound they made caused a loud bang inside my head and was driving me insane. A blinding pulse of light dazed through my head every second. Then all of a sudden, everything stopped. I thought I had turned deaf. But it was just quiet. I tried to gather my thoughts and concentrate on what was happening. All the kids were standing around me. They had a sad look on their faces. They were looking at me like an animal in a zoo. At least, they looked concerned for me. They looked sad for me.

But I was wrong. I was very wrong.

They suddenly let out a huge and cheerful scream. I could not understand what had caused the sudden reaction. They seemed happy as if they had found something important. I was a fool - I thought they were happy to see me. I thought they, may be, recognized me. But then the horror of what was happening struck me like a bolt. They brought a long rope and tied it to my legs. I tried to resist. At the other end of the rope was a garland cracker. It was made of ten thousand tiny little crackers that would continue to burst for a few minutes. I was not going to imagine what was going to happen. They were going to the light the cracker. That was a long cracker and I was sure I was not going to last the entirety of the bursting crackers.

I begged them to stop but they did not. I screamed, I pleaded with them. But all of that fell on deaf ears. They made fun of me. They taunted me. I had no other option but to fight back. I was never a fighter. I never before had the need to fight. I struggled under the grips of the stronger children. One thing led to another and I snapped. I did not know what happened. I certainly did not know.

One of the kids who was holding me stopped laughing. He screamed all of a sudden. I did not know what I had done but I certainly knew he was screaming in pain. I saw blood rushing from his arm. I didn't know how but in some weird way I had hurt him.

They all stopped playing and gathered around the bleeding kid. Their screaming had stopped and they all went eerily quiet. They were giving all the attention to the kid. I, for a second, thought they were going to let me go. That's the way the world worked, I thought - stomp on the downtrodden hoping they would not fight back. I was very sure I had scared the hell out of them. I was sure I had escaped the ordeal. But I knew I was wrong again when they all turned around to see me.

I did not understand till the first heavy stone hit me on the shoulder. It was immensely painful. Another stone came straight to my face but I dodged it. And then one too many stones came from all directions and I could not escape any of them. I wobbled face first unable to feel my legs. I was sure something was broken. I waited for the pain to settle down but there were more and more injuries every second. I was unable to move and I took every hit on my body.

One of the huge rocks hit me on the side of my head. It sent a surge of shock waves to my brain. I could feel the blood pouring out of my head. The blood covered my already blurred vision. My consciousness slowly wore away. The burden was too much to bear and I almost gave up.

My story now, or whatever that is left of it...

As my eyes begin to close and my vision goes dark, I think of the happy moments of my life. They seem like far and distant memories. But the little memories of my little family; my mom and my dad are bright.

I am down on the ground and I try to see through the blur. I can see a few people running towards me but I do not want to find out if they are going to inflict more pain or if they are coming to help. I have no energy to wait for them. I decide to finally give up. There is nothing more for me to even decide. I give up.

And in these final moments a few questions come to my mind.

What did I do to deserve an end like this?

Was it because I was born poor?

Was it because I was an orphan?

Or was it because… ***I was just a dog*?**

Code Name: MAKAIBARI

Memories Of The Blue Eyes

Code Name: MAKAIBARI

Security Clearance Level: F2A9Z66

Description: This is an agency level transcript of the audio file recovered from Agent Number 80928 with clear security restrictions. Names, locations, keywords and phrases have been redacted for security reasons.

Audio Date: 11th of June 2015

Transcription Date: 15th of June 2015

Transcript begins------------------------

As I always begin my audio diary recordings, my name is ███████ - Agent Number 80928. The audio is encrypted to agency standards. If decryption is attempted without the required algorithm, the file will self-destruct. If you are listening to this, I am quite sure I am no longer alive, either the guilt was enough for me to put a bullet to my head or someone beat me to it.

I work for the government of course. Not with the ███████ as most of the people would have heard over and over in countless films and read in a million books. Actually, I don't work for any agency that exists on paper. Only four of us who are the employees of this particular agency and only one government liaison know of our existence – he would, of course, remain unnamed.

My IQ is off the charts. Sheldon Cooper, Harold Finch if you know who they are, would kill to have my IQ. I thought I was going to change the world with my level of knowledge and intelligence. I am doing it, in one weird sense. Not in a way I would have wanted to or imagined I could – but changing the world, nevertheless.

I have never had any friends when I grew up in ███████. Neither do I have any friends or family now. The sole purpose of my existence is the agency and the work I do. Other than that, all I know are the women I sleep with every now and then – biological urges, you see. I have seen their faces once and never again and I don't want to.

My contract with the agency says I am a 'Strategist'. I, sometimes, find that funny because I think it should say 'Assassin'. You heard me right, I kill people for a living. That's what all the four of us do at the agency – we kill people. No, neither do we use guns or any weapons nor do we kill in the conventional sense. But we do, I more than the others. I have always outsmarted the others and my success rate is far higher than all of theirs put together.

I travel on the ▇▇▇▇▇▇▇▇ train line every day to my place of work in ▇▇▇▇▇▇▇▇. To call it an office would be an insult to a real office. It's more of a garage with some peculiarly fancy but state of the art equipment. It looks more often like a mad scientist's laboratory that was just broken to pieces by a chimp.

'So, what does a crazy strategist like me do?' you may ask. 'Nothing!' most days. Sometimes weeks and months go by without us having to do anything at all. I just read, read, and read to satiate the brain of such high IQ – it's like feeding a packet of popcorn to the super hungry elephant. The world changes every day and the knowledge and updated information are the keys to the complex and messed up system. But the world changes too slowly in my opinion.

And then, after almost months, the phone would ring on a secure line. Very meagre details would be shared over the phone – mostly just a name. And if we are lucky, a place related to the name. Within minutes of the phone call, a shit load of data would be dumped on us. Data that's supposed to look like shit to anyone one else but us.

To us, hiding in that shit load of data somewhere would be the tiny little key to killing whoever it was.

I had no serious timelines to work against. I had to get rid of the target and I did before anyone asked me the second time. I hate to be asked the second time. That's how good I was. I was a genius and it would not take long to find the needle in the haystack - a clearly shining needle in the heaps of dull and rotten hay. And all I would have to do was to poison the needle in the easiest possible ways.

Almost every evening, I would find a woman for company - just for the night. No strings attached in any stupid way. Simple and pure fun to keep the engine running. Did I say women were my distraction? I did, didn't I? Oh yeah! I don't try to hide that like the other men do. After all, who did I have to save face for? Women - distraction - simple and basic biology. Even talking about women has distracted me - Sorry, back to what I was talking about.

So, I tidy up the data to the bare minimum to find a very minor and basic detail - a needle in a haystack. And once that is found, it's all pretty simple.

Let me give you an example. One of my recent targets was ▇▇▇▇▇▇▇▇▇▇▇ Yes, the famous rebel leader from that little island country that was in the news recently, ▇▇▇▇▇▇▇▇▇▇▇

I was given the name.

I was given the data.

There had been various counter-intelligence operations for many a year to get the motherfucker killed. Bullets, missiles, bombs, he had dodged them all. He had four look-alikes as far as the data showed. They were always in line to take the hit. He had, even more, people to protect him. He had guards on alert round the clock, only his son was allowed to get in the physical distance with him. He had even dodged poisoned food many times. He would be the whole deal in the book on 'How to escape an assassination', if it was written that is.

So, I ▇▇▇▇▇▇▇▇▇, with that extremely fucked up brain of mine had to find a solution.

When I said 'Tea' was my answer, everyone laughed. It was so simple and funny when I mentioned it. But it needed a lot of explanation and work. Then, they all got it. It was fucking brilliant, in my opinion, and bloody serious.

The target drank inhuman amounts of tea every single day - bucket loads was an understatement. It was a specific brand of tea picked, procured, processed and packed specially for him. All we had to do was change one package among the dozens that were brought to his house. The package still was tea - the same tea that he loved but with a little additive that I discovered. In simpler terms, a poison specifically designed to match him. To be more precise, match his rare blood group factoring in his age and the regular amounts of the tea he drank.

So, there was no date when he would die. It all depended on when that particular package of tea was used. He was definitely going to die without any suspicion. The autopsy would most possibly say he suffered a heart attack. Twenty-three days was all it took. They were trying to kill him for fourteen-fucking-years.

Once he was dead, there was a 'staged' uprising and after the loss of thousands of lives, and with some heavy-duty media coverage, a dummy selected by our very own government was elected to be the next in line - all in a short span of twelve weeks.

So, that's what I do. I am a strategist. Or should I say, 'I was' given the fact that I would be dead by the time this audio is available to listen. Doesn't matter, does it?

No one really knows who I am. Not the hot redhead living upstairs, not the person who serves me lunch every day at two pm, not the short bald guy standing in front of me now waiting for the elevator. He's probably thinking I am talking on my phone. If he had paid attention, he would have noticed there was no signal in this part of the station – that's how much of common sense prevailed in the world nowadays. The routine checks on my name by the agency had not shown any red spots in the most recent run – still safe is what I have been told.

But... I have got my fears. Once you have gotten a job like mine, it was only a matter of time. Once you are spotted, they will move in as quickly as an eagle pouncing on a field rat. One minute, I am just a guy with a beard in the middle of a huge crowd and the next, I could be a dead man. Things could escalate that quickly.

That fear apart, there is this conscience that would play the sad guilt track occasionally. When you look closer and closer the plain simple truth is that I kill people. Someone's dad or someone's son or someone's all powerful but loving grandfather or someone who could unite an entire clan of people with his or her thoughts and words. They could be termed as revolutionaries, guerrillas, terrorists or whatever. But they were human beings in one sense or the other and that guilt would still play its part at some point or the other.

Except for those women in my life who I don't really know, there was nothing. Nothing close and nothing to lose. I don't feel lonely, though – fuck no. It's all... What's the word I am looking for... Well, sufficient. It's all sufficient.

It's all going well except that the sense of fear and guilt had been a touch too much to handle in the last few days. A person like me needs to trust his instincts and I do – Which is why I believe I am in real danger.

The train station is extra busy today and I think there are going to be delays on the way. I can see swarms of people trying to get into the little available space on the platform – it's going to be a long ride home, I think. My attempt to squeeze through the crowd ended in a failure but then this sudden standstill of people seems to have worked in my favour.

I see her. Amidst the boring mass of people, I see her.

A bright red dress to tell the world that she is to be noticed. She is slim, tall and for the lack of a better way to describe her – super sexy. She could easily be the next Bond girl in whatever Daniel Craig decides to do after Skyfall. Maybe she is the girl Daniel Craig leaves Rachel Weisz for. She is that hot. Every man walking down the stairs is looking at her.

Women are a distraction – I warned you! This woman is indeed a distraction. I can't even think clearly when I am looking at her. God, I can hardly breathe. I am sure the blood supply to the brain is so limited at this minute. No guessing for where the blood is rushing now. If you still need a clue, think gravity. What a perfection of a woman!

She walks like a bird with her high heels barely touching the floor. I can see her skin shining. Even if the sun closes its eyes now she would still glow like gold. The way her hand slides on the handrail is poetic. Every step she takes gives me an erotic shudder through my heart and mind.

I drag my hand on the handrail, just like her. I think I really need to hold it as it was getting a bit too much and my knees could give up anytime. I look at her. She is coming closer to me on the other side of the handrail. I really need some air!

Our eyes just meet – she has cool blue eyes. Really? Blue eyes? It did not match her beauty or her dress or hair. Such out of place eyes! Those horrible eyes look like they don't even belong to her! Weird!

Just as she crosses me, her hand brushes against mine. I feel a surge of electric current – I promise I am not dreaming. It sure felt like a touch of static! A stupid feeling, I know. And then, she disappeared. Just like that. I don't even remember the episode now. It was all too quick!

What a distraction that was!

I do feel a bit sad that it was all over too quick. My elevated heart beat has returned to normal. I was breathing heavily for those few seconds when she was so close to me in that crowded mass of people. But, the breathing is normal now. Thinking about it and more I think about it, my breathing is getting slower.

God! Was it so much excitement that I am running out of breath? My body is shaking and my vision is getting blurry as I speak. And I can see the people around me looking at me with concern.

One of the guys is pointing at something on my arm. It has taken me a few seconds to understand what he is saying and I look at my arm. My vision is blurry but I can see what he is saying. There is a little cut on the spot where she had brushed past me and I can see a spreading patch of blue - spreading faster than my vision can adjust. Damn! I was distracted so much that I missed her completely. She was my fear come true!

I don't think my legs can hold me anymore and I am stumbling more and more. The people around me are not trying to help me - maybe they are scared. They maintain a safe distance and I can see a couple of good Samaritans screaming for help. The next thing I realise is stumbling off the platform and falling onto the tracks. I can see a bright light approaching me. It is getting brighter and brighter.

Transcript ends------------------------

A cup of tea in the Irish Pub

Mike woke up to the sound of the screaming alarm. It was Christmas Eve of the year 2011. It was far later in the day for anyone to wake up to an alarm. He woke up feeling light headed, not that it was unusual. He had felt the same way for quite a few years.

The sound of the alarm was increasing after every ten seconds and the sound was becoming unbearable. He had to get the bloody thing switched off. The alarm was on his left at a pretty reachable distance. All he had to do was to move his left arm and switch the alarm off – that was if he could.

He wished he could sense his arm. He wished he could move his left arm a little bit. He wished the same every single day when he opened his eyes in the morning. But that was not going to be the case. That was never going to be the case.

He left the alarm ringing. It would stop eventually tired of waiting for someone to switch it off. It was not going to bother him because his mind was in a place far, far away where everything was back to how it was – back to when music and happiness were the only things in his life.

Part I – The Guitar

'Next on stage...', the announcement came. The silence was immense.

'...the man who is going to play with your heart in the same way he is going to play with the strings of his guitar...', he continued.

And, just like the rain pouring down without a hint of drizzle, the crowd roared with an inexplicable enthusiasm and

Memories Of The Blue Eyes

unbelievable frenzy. He was the man who everyone in the crowd was waiting for. And, this was the thirty minutes that every one of them had come there for.

It was the 23rd of December 2007, the last night of the ten-day music festival. And, in the same way all the music festivals were planned, the last night was always the best. Given that it was the Christmas holiday week the concert was packed. And the best of the best was this thirty minutes. The thirty minutes with Michael Harris – and his guitar, of course.

Mike took the stage. His eyes were closed and the silence was stunning. Slowly, his fingers moved like a feather over the strings of the guitar. The plectrum was striking the strings so smoothly that it could hardly be noticed. It looked as though his fingers were performing a ballet on the fret and ice dancing on the strings - beautifully coordinated movements. The serpent tattoo on his hand danced gloriously to his tunes.

The music was, in short, heavenly. Every time Mike struck the strings of his guitar, everyone in the crowd felt their heart strings pulled. The music was emotional. Like all the times when Mike played in a concert, it was music for the heart rather than the mind. That was what made Mike everyone's favourite.

'It was an evening filled with music that could only be produced by a brilliant guitarist on a classical instrument. Michael Harris performed with utmost charm and perfection', were going to be the lines in most of the magazines.

Michael Harris loved his guitar more than anything else. His grandfather presented him with a classy black guitar when he was twelve. Little did he know he had such a talent in him till he started strumming the guitar for the first time? From that day on, there was no turning back. It was just a matter of time before he was adored.

Mike never believed in learning music and he never tried. He always felt that music was part of the soul. His music was always from the heart and it was a spontaneous wave that connected the mind and body. There were a number of requests for him to teach music but he would frankly say he did not know or believe in teaching music.

'I find the squiggly designs quite confusing', he would say referring to the musical notes. He could be one of those undocumented cases of the savant syndrome.

The concert was quite a success and it was time for Michael to get home. He called his brother Tom. He was the one who was supposed to pick him up after the concert.

'I will pick you up at eleven near the Spanish bar', Tom had said when Mike left home for the concert.

Mike tried a few times but there was no answer. The calls kept reaching the voicemail. It got him a little irritated. It was very late. He had to travel all the way to Reading and the last train from London Paddington was at eleven forty-five. He would have to take the Circle or Hammersmith and City line from Hammersmith to Paddington. He had only a few minutes to get the train.

He packed his guitar in its case and started jogging toward the Hammersmith underground station. The station looked devoid of any activity. He had reached the station just in time for the train at eleven twenty and boarded it just in time for the train doors to close. The train was almost empty but for one girl at the far corner of the coach. She was either drunk or half asleep. She was dressed in glittering black and looked like she was returning from a party of some sort.

Michael did not show much interest in the girl. He placed his guitar near him. He had his eyes closed for a few minutes as the train reached the Latimer Road station. He never felt alone because music was there for company. Music was something that he thought about all the time. The tunes that he had played, the tunes that he had planned to play. He never noted them down in any way. He could play any tune he was asked for.

When he was asked about how his mind and music gel together, he would smile, tap his forehead and quote Andy Dufresne from Shawshank Redemption, *'That's the beauty of music. They can't get that from you. Haven't you ever felt that way about music?'*

His mind was on the interlude he would be playing at the church for the Christmas Eve mass. He loved the church where he had gone all his life. People loved his music there too. His interlude for the communion was as special as Christmas itself. He was playing his interlude over and over in his mind. He for one knew that it was going to be adored by everyone.

Part II – The Girl

He had a few more stations to go but thought he would get to Paddington just in time for his train to Reading. Just as the train doors were about to close, a group of three young chaps boarded the train. They were visibly drunk.

People, under the influence of alcohol, travelling in the London underground trains was not unusual. Mike went back to his music – that heavenly music that was going to mesmerize everyone in the church. It would have been a few minutes when the train came to halt underground in the tunnel – probably waiting for the signal to turn green at the next station. There was silence for a few seconds and something disturbed him. He turned to the girl.

The guys who had boarded the train were getting into an argument with the girl. For a moment, he thought of minding his own business. As a matter of fact, people got into trouble with drunkards one way or the other. But something did not seem right. When he was about to get back to what he was doing, one of the guys did something to the girl which he should never have. The guy did something that got him to his breaking point.

'Leave her alone!', Mike shouted from where he was.

One of the guys turned back swearing and shouting at Mike to mind his own business. But Mike was not someone who could be scared off. Mike picked up his guitar and walked towards them.

'I said, Leave the girl alone!', he insisted.

The three guys turned their attention on Mike. They were pretty well built and looked strong. But they knew so little about Mike that their strong looks were not going to intimidate him. Besides his musical and easy-going life, Mike had a serious interest in martial arts and self-defense. It looked like this was going to be the perfect time to put his non-musical skills to test.

The guy swore at Mike again and told him to shut up. When Mike kept walking towards them, he took a wild swing in the direction of Mike who was already on the alert. He ducked the punch and landed a strong close distance jab that, in words that echoed in many of the Rocky Balboa films, would have rattled his ancestors. The guy would have felt a shriek of pain through his ribs and in his spine. He fell like a weasel.

Seeing one of his mates being hit enraged the others. The second guy pounced towards Mike who casually moved a couple of steps back. The guy crashed on the train floor. Mike quickly jabbed him strongly in his back, just below his neck. Mike knew that it would keep the guy quiet for a while. The last one was left baffled and he looked far too feeble than the others. Mike stared at him which was enough to make him fall to his knees. Mike walked past him to the girl to ensure she was alright.

'Are you alright?', he asked her. She was visibly shaken by the unexpected turn of events. She nodded to say she was ok. She was ready to break into tears any second.

'You poor thing', Mike thought. He turned back to the guys who were still on the floor. It did not look like they were going to get into another fight for some time. They would think a lot before troubling anyone again.

The train came to a stop at Bayswater station. When the train door opened, the guy who had escaped Mike's beating ran out like mad, literally scared. Mike smiled and turned to the girl. She looked fine and he was sure there was a smile about to break anytime soon.

'I am Michael Harris.', he said extending his hand in a friendly gesture.

'Sarah Sanchez', she said shaking his hand.

'Thanks a lot for...', she was searching for the right word.

'Well, thanks for everything', she said pointing to the guys who were beaten up.

Part III – The Pain

Mike continued to smile, not willing to let go of her hand but had to before it looked awkward. But before that the train came to a squealing halt at Paddington. He had to get down and of all probability will have to run to get the train home. There was something in her smile that felt so peaceful. It was not the ordinary smile that a guy would see in a girl. That smile seemed to say, *'You've got a friend in me'*.

'Here's my stop', said Mike to which surprisingly she said, *'Mine too!'*

Both of them smiled and got down from the train. Just as he took a step away from the train, he realised he had forgotten something.

'Oh my...! I forgot my guitar' he said. He got back into the train feeling a little strange. This was the first time that he had ever forgotten his guitar. First time ever!

'I blame it on her', he said to himself. He picked up the guitar but unfortunately the doors of the train were already

closing. He stepped out in time but his left hand was caught between the train doors with his guitar inside.

'Oh, fuck!', he cursed.

Obviously, the safety mechanisms of the London underground trains did not allow the train to move unless all the doors were closed. People got stuck at the doors all the time and it would be just a matter of time before the operator would open the doors again. Mike waited. The doors did not open. The operator was just taking his time thought Mike. Sarah waited behind him.

In the London underground, the far end of the platform where the operator's cabin stopped, there usually was a huge mirror. It acted as a rear-view mirror for the operator to ensure that no one is blocking the doors or to avoid any mishaps when the train started moving. Michael waved towards the mirror in a hurry trying to grab the operator's attention. Both of them were looking curiously trying to understand why in the world the operator was taking a lot of time.

With all their attention focused in the operator's direction, both of them failed to notice the movement within the train. At an unexpected moment, someone wildly pulled Mike from inside the train. This caught him completely off guard.

One of the guys who Mike had neutralised in the train earlier was now awake. He was pulling Mike's hand from inside. Mike tried wedging the train doors open to get back into the train so that he could give it back. The doors would not budge. The guy was furious and his eyes were burning with anger. He was clearly out for revenge.

Mike was not intimidated. He never was. At least not until the guy pulled out a knife from his jacket. It looked like no ordinary knife. Unbeknownst to Mike, it was a heavy-duty hunting knife. The specialty of those kinds of knives was minimum impact and maximum damage. The blade cut through the target on the way in and the serrated edges tore the flesh on the way out - *Minimum impact - Maximum damage.*

Michael Harris' face lost colour. And, Sarah began to scream.

The first stab tore through the triceps. The knife neatly cut through all the way to the bone. When it came out rupturing everything in its way along with the spurting fountain of blood, all Mike could do was to scream.

Sarah ran away screaming for help. She screamed and screamed, for what seemed to be, forever.

The second stab was even stronger because it did not stop just at the bone but went on to break it. Then there was the third and fourth and so on. It seemed like a psychopathic rage and it did not end till the thirteenth stab when Mike blacked out.

Just before Mike blacked out he saw a blurred image of Sarah running towards him. There were a few people running behind her for help. The doors of the train finally opened and he fell unconscious to the ground in a pool of his own blood. But his fingers, knowingly or unknowingly, were still tightly holding on to his guitar case. Amidst the rush of immense pain and loss of blood, Mike did not know that he had not felt any of the stabs halfway through the rampage. And he did not know that it was the last time his left arm would ever hold on to his dear guitar.

Deep down in his mind, the interlude for Christmas Eve kept playing over and over.

The police and ambulance arrived at the scene and Mike was carried away to the hospital. He had suffered thirteen stab wounds in total and four of them were compound fractures. He had also suffered a heavy loss of blood. He was unconscious all the time. The two guys had escaped before anyone could realise. Police were investigating the CCTV footages in the train as well as the Paddington station and they were quite sure they would get them.

Sarah had accompanied Mike in tears all the way to the hospital. His parents, John and Margaret Harris were called and informed of the situation. They reached the hospital in an hour's time. Sarah waited for them in the hospital. When his mother arrived at the ICU, Sarah burst into tears.

'It was my fault. I should never have been there. I got him into this', she cried. *'I never expected anything of this sort to happen'*, she continued in a teary guilt-ridden voice.

Given the situation, John and Margaret were upset but were steady. They had gone through a lot in life and they had stood by each other through all storms and quakes. *'This too shall pass'*, they would say. John brought Sarah a cup of coffee while Margaret sat down consoling Sarah.

'Don't you worry love, Mikey will be alright', Margaret said patting Sarah on her cheek. Sarah saw a gem of a woman in Margaret.

'I am sorry Mrs. Harris.', Sarah said and burst into tears again. But all the three of them sat there waiting for Mike to be brought out of the operation theatre. Sarah felt a sensitive wave of understanding with Mike and his family; a family who could remain so brave amidst adversities.

John kept trying to reach Tom all night till he received a call back. Tom had been partying at the Irish bar and had forgotten all about Mike. When he heard the news, he was shell shocked and immediately got to the hospital.

When Mike woke up in the morning, his vision still blurred and with an overwhelming nausea, he immediately sensed something was wrong. Before he could understand what it was, he threw up. In the next few minutes he fell unconscious. He was in the same state for the next forty hours. It was the effect of the heavy sedation and the loss of blood the doctors explained. Theoretically there was nothing to worry about. Well, theoretically.

He woke up a little more stabilised on the third day. It was Boxing Day. He had missed Christmas that year, spending the day in a quasi-stable state. The world looked slightly brighter and things looked a little clearer that morning. He could see his parents, his brother and the girl from the train waiting eagerly for him at his bedside. But his eyes did not stop searching until Sarah pointed to his guitar. Only then did he smile weakly.

The happiness and the feeling of relief in the room were immense. But, the happiness was short lived. The consultant who was on rounds came over to talk to Mike. And, it took only a minute for Mike to realise there was something very wrong.

'Doing alright, Mr. Harris?', asked the consultant to which Mike gave a tired nod in agreement.

'How is your arm and are you in pain?', asked the consultant.

'Pain, what pain?', asked Mike and looked at his arm. The left arm was completely bandaged after the operation. There were six plates used to hold his broken bones together. There were a hundred and eighty-two stitches in total to cover the stab wounds. But, Mike could not feel even a hint of pain in his entire left arm.

'I am sorry...?', asked the consultant in a very confused tone.

'Doctor...', said Mike in a trembling voice.

'Doctor, I can't feel my arm', he gasped. That was the end of everything as Mike knew it.

Part IV – The Agony

'You can take my life but not my music!' – words of an ancient musician. These words, according to history, were said by the musician before he was executed. The emperor had ordered the execution because he could muster so many people when he performed than when the emperor himself spoke. When the musician was given the choices of not to perform anymore or be executed, he chose the latter.

60

If Mike had been given the choice, he would have happily followed the footsteps of that musician. But, without even a slightest hint, it was all taken away. His fingers would never feel the strings of the guitar again. They were not going to dance with the strings again. His left arm was never going to feel the guitar again.

The doctors initially explained that it would be the effect of the sedation, rupture of the nerves, and all other possible causes. Minutes, hours, days and weeks went by without any indication of improvement. One by one, the doctors lost hope followed by the family and friends of Mike and lastly Mike himself. Something more terrible than the pain when the knife tore his muscles had become a reality. That pain would have eventually ceased to exist but this would just remain stuck to his heart.

After nearly three months of medical ordeals, the case of Michael Harris was considered one of those to remain unsolved. The wounds had healed and all the medical tests showed a perfectly functioning arm but that was not the case in reality. The arm stayed dead for all practical purposes. And slowly as days became months, everyone had lost hope.

The world around Mike began to shrink day by day. The more he lost hope, the more it became smaller. Initially there were a lot of people who came over to console him. There would be a lot of letters, flowers and cards outside his house for him to get well soon.

The flowers dried up, the letters and cards became rubbish. And so did the people. The people who followed his music were no longer there. His girlfriend for three years did not bother to come back after a few weeks.

'That's how the world is son', John and Margaret would try to console him.

And the worst part was Mike had trouble understanding himself. His mind seemed to be working far too differently when it was away from music. The man in the mirror was no longer the Michael Harris everyone knew. He was not the same person he himself knew.

He confined himself to his own room. Some days he would just keep crying until his eyes dried up. Sometimes he would just stare at his guitar for hours on end. He would rush to a music concert or listen to his own musical recordings but every single second would remind him of his inability which drove him mad. Finally, he lost trust in God.

He had nightmares of the day when he was stabbed and had to struggle putting himself to sleep. He would wake up in the middle of the night gasping for breath. He rarely stepped out of the house. Even if he did, he would walk aimlessly around the streets. The thought of the London underground train made him dizzy and a sense of nausea set in.

Amidst the ordeal, there were only four people who stuck with him - His parents John and Margaret, his brother Tom and the girl from the train, Sarah. But the relationship was not as healthy as before. The one and only time that he had talked to Tom was a week after the incident. That too it was just a harsh accusatory sentence – *'You should have picked me up'*. That accusation was enough and it was the last time he met Tom's eyes. All the encounters after that were Tom's apologies when Mike was staring into the void.

Sarah would visit the family every other week. Whatever work she had or wherever she was, she would drop by. She would help Margaret with the household stuff, take a lot of John's advice and had a friend in Tom. But Mike stayed in his own world and the guilt of which Sarah had to live with, for what looked like, forever.

And it had been four years ever since. Mike had forgotten all about his music. His mind was as dead as his left arm. The interlude he had in his mind for the Christmas of 2007 was the only piece of music he remembered. The pain of the knife was short lived but the agony was going with Mike to the grave.

Part V - Christmas Eve

Mike woke up to the sound of his screaming alarm. It was Christmas Eve of 2011. It was far later in the day for anyone to wake up to an alarm. He woke up feeling light headed – not that it was unusual. He had felt the same way for quite a few years now.

There was a soft knock on the door. It was his mother. Mike did not answer but Margaret brought him breakfast with a steaming cup of tea.

'I am not hungry', said Mike with his mind lost in space.

A mother knew when her son was hungry and she did not have to be told. Mike was just trying to avoid her presence in his room, in his world. That was not going to defer her away. She wanted to be with Mike all the time and take care of him. Every single minute, all these four years, all she wanted to see was her Mike to be back to normal. She had decided to speak up today.

'Mike...', she said. She waited for a response or acknowledgement but there was none.

'Mike, I know it's been a difficult few years for you', Margaret continued.

'Difficult...?', burst Mike. *'How bad can difficult be when I have lost everything?'*

Margaret was quiet for a few minutes. The situation had been the same with Mike however much she had tried to talk to him. She and John had made sure that he was not bothered so much but looked like she had to talk to him again as his situation was getting worse by the day.

'I know it was everything for you Mikey', said Margaret taking her time on her next words.

'And, I know difficult is not the right word. But...', she waited and slowly tears appeared at the corners of her eyes. And, just to assure her, John stepped inside the room. Margaret could not control her tears. John put his arm around her shoulder as she stood up to leave.

'I may not know how you feel Mikey. But we feel as if we have lost our son', John said.

'And you don't know how it feels to have lost a son', John said firmly and walked slowly out of the room with Margaret.

Mike was left alone again in his room and his anger slowly subsided. His tears had dried off. The whole encounter with his parents seemed surreal up until his father had spoken. Something had hit him very strongly. After a long four years he had realised that not only was he affected but his loss has affected a lot of people.

Mike spent the entire afternoon sleeping. His mind went over his father's words again and again. And then, a voice spoke to him from inside.

'Move on Mike'

'Get over it Mike. Wake up!'

'It is enough, Mikey!'

Mike was startled and woke up breathing heavily. Something in him felt different. He waited till his breathing settled down. He opened the windows and took in a fresh breath of air. And, after a huge sigh, his world looked slightly brighter. He went out of his room to see his parents.

He walked out to the hall. He had not noticed the Christmas tree all these days. It was so beautiful – just as his life once was. John and Margaret were seated on the sofa. It was clear that Margaret had been crying. They looked up at their son. It had been ages since he had walked into the hall to meet them face to face.

'I am…', Mike blurted out. He did not have the courage and energy to speak up.

'…sorry', he said.

And without a moment's hesitation he sank into his mom and dad's shoulders and cried and cried. He cried like a little child. Margaret and John let him cry it all out. They were there for him and wished they would get back their son. It took Mike a very long time to cry it out.

And when he stopped, he did not know what to say and said, *'I am sorry for everything'*.

It was Christmas and it was the time for things to change for the better. John helped Mike get ready for the Christmas Eve mass. It was entirely different to see his son clean shaven with his now longer hair neatly gelled in a formal Christmas suit. Mike had thinned down a lot and the suit was slightly big for him but nevertheless he looked adorable – again.

In an apologetic tone Mike said, *'Merry Christmas mom and dad'*. There was a moment of silence before which John and Margaret hugged their son with all their heart and with their eyes filled with tears of happiness.

They reached the church for the Christmas Eve mass. There were a lot of surprised looks when Michael walked in. A lot of people turned around and recognized him. A few people who he knew waved to him from the far corners.

'People have not forgotten you', John whispered to Mike.

The surprise of seeing their favourite guitarist Michael Harris was very genuine. Their smiles were not only on their lips but in their eyes as well. Mike never thought the world would remember him but he was wrong. For the first time in a very long four years, a weak smile emerged from the corner of his lips.

Part VI – The interlude... again

Christmas at his parish church had always been bright and beautiful. That year, after a long gap, it felt brighter than ever before. The colours were vibrant, the decorations were heavenly and the alignment of candles around the church was stunning. It was a beautiful place and a wonderful time for Mike to get better memories– a place to forget the worst.

He patiently sat through the entire mass and prayers. The choir was at its best. The music reminded him of a lot but for some good reason, his mind seemed to adjust to it and not go back into his past. The songs and music were in a way mesmerising. The violin played a wonderful part all through the first few songs. And, it was time for the communion. People started queuing for the Holy Communion and Mike stepped to the queue followed by his parents.

All seemed to be normal till something startled him. Out of the blue, he heard the sound of a guitar. His thoughts went back to the interlude that he had planned to play for the Christmas Eve mass long back. His mind went back to playing that piece of music. It was not just some ordinary music from the guitar. It was a heavenly tune which could mesmerise anyone.

He tried to shake his head and get the music out of his mind. He did not want to go back to whatever it was. He stood still for a second in the middle of the moving queue and waited with his hands on his forehead. He tried and tried but he could not. The music kept playing. And then a realisation struck him. It was not the music playing in his mind. Someone was actually playing it. Someone was actually playing the music – his music. It was the music from his mind and someone was playing it in the very church he was in.

Mike went pale. He eyes lost life and if anyone had seen him at that very moment, they would have thought that he had seen a ghost.

'It's not possible...', he muttered to himself. It was such a shock that he was shivering. His shirt was soaked with sweat and his knees were going to buckle in any second.

'How in the world...?', he continued his questions to himself.

John nudged from behind asking him to keep moving in the queue. Amidst the shock and shivering, it was impossible for Mike to keep moving. The thing about all his music was that he never could write them down or note them down. He played his music from his mind. Always. There was not a speck of chance that someone could have heard this piece of music. He had composed it in his mind and had not even had the chance to play it once.

'This can't be true', he kept mumbling as he walked forward.

The choir slowly came into view. The violinist was waiting for the guitarist to finish. The singers were looking at the guitarist, probably mesmerised. The people seated in the front rows were all looking in the direction of the choir, probably mesmerised too. The music was indeed heavenly.

Mike tried to see the face of the guitarist but it was in the shadow of the decorated arch. The silhouette was blurred in the bright lights around. All Mike could see was the guitar and fingers playing with the strings. It was a lovely black guitar – just like his. The fingers moved with such a style and the strings vibrated with such elegance. The fingernails were painted in pink and a beautiful tattoo of a serpent gracing her arm. The serpent seemed to dance gloriously to the music. Just like the serpent tattoo on his hand did years before.

Mike tried his best to see the guitarist's face but he could not. The fingers kept elegantly playing the guitar but he could not move away from his queue. He was almost guided all the way back to his seat. His eyes were fixed in the direction of the choir though he could not see them from where he was.

'I need to see the guitarist', he said to Margaret and John.

'Mikey, you can't move around now. It's time for the final blessing', he was told.

Mike could not resist and wait till the mass was over but he had no choice. After the final prayers, the priests made their walk back down the aisle following the cross. Mike simply did not have the patience and John almost had to leash him back just to avoid things looking odd. Finally, when he got the chance, he ran across the aisle dragging his arm along to the choir box. His old friend James Hilton was the choir leader now.

'Is that you Mike? How the devil are you?', he asked with his feverishly enthusiastic voice.

'I am...', muttered Mike.

'I am fine, James', he continued nervously. *'Eh, I was searching for the guitarist'*.

James could not understand what the question was or why but he clearly saw the nervousness in Mike's voice.

'The guitarist?', asked James.

'I don't know, I just heard the music. Can you just tell me where he is?'

'It's a she not he. The guitarist who played today was a girl. Did you not see her?', James continued.

'Ok, where is she?'

'She left through the back door for the choir', James said pointing to the door.

'Ah, why didn't you say this first', thought Mike but said *'Thank you'* instead. He rushed to the door. When he reached the parking lot near the door, his eyes were wildly searching for the girl.

He finally found her. But not before she kept her bright silver guitar case into the taxi and got in. Mike ran towards the taxi waving and asking the driver to hold on but amidst the crowd and the Christmas enthusiasm the taxi did not stop.

Mike stood there with his right hand on his knee and his left hand hanging from his shoulder gasping for breath. It was too much to take for him. Things were starting to blur again.

'It can't be true', he kept repeating. His heart was in an inexplicable enthusiasm combined with a grip of confusion. Someone by some unbeknownst power and reason had played a piece of music from his mind. Somewhere someone shared his waves of music.

John and Margaret came to him after searching for him in the church.

'Are you alright, Mikey?', Margaret asked fearing for the worst.

Mike took his time to calm down. When his breathing became normal, he looked up at his parents with happiness shining in his eyes.

'My music...', he stammered with happiness.

'My music is alive', he said.

Part VII – The girl with the serpent tattoo

It was difficult to explain the situation to his parents. But when he finally did, the relief and happiness in their faces was immense. They could see the light at the end of the tunnel. Finally, there was some hope in their son's life. After all the suffering, he had made a musical connection.

'It's too late to do anything about this Mikey', John said. *'But trust me, we will find her'*.

Mike had always wanted to finish things and had problems in waiting for a solution. His level of patience was less compared to others. From having talked to his parish priest and James Hilton, they could just get the girl's name and where she had come from. But that was not going to satisfy Mike. His impatience was growing every second. He had trouble sleeping that night. Well, he had had trouble sleeping for quite a few years but this was different. This was really very different.

He woke up very early but had nothing to do or nowhere to go for the time being. It was Christmas but it was going to be a quiet day with almost every indoors having a feast with their beloved families.

'Mike, you are not going anywhere dear. We are going to have our Christmas lunch today as a family', Margaret had said.

Tom and Sarah arrived just when John was helping Mike with something. Tom had not been told about the situation. He almost choked on his chewing gum and Sarah stood breathless when they saw a different Mike in the room. The aura of happiness in the room was immense.

'Merry Christmas, Tom', Michael wished Tom who was still unsure of what was happening.

'Merry Christmas, Sarah', he said and she gave him a big hug filled with happiness.

Mike immediately sensed something unusual. He looked at Sarah and Tom with a smile. As they stood lost in their smiles, Mike asked, *'What did I miss?'*

Sarah blushed and leaned on Tom's shoulder and replied, *'Not a lot, I think'*

One of the things that Mike had not known was that Tom and Sarah had been in love with each other for over a year now. They were each other's consolation when people worried long about Mike. Tom had moved in with Sarah about six months back. Margaret stood in the kitchen watching everything. She had not spoken but her tears spoke a million words – words of happiness. Her son was back after four long years and she could see her happy family.

It was going to be a Merry Christmas indeed.

'So, it's a girl, huh?', Tom asked when he was savouring the dessert. Michael nodded.

'Her name is Christina Sahayaraj. She is a guitarist from the West Ham parish church'

'West Ham parish, you say? What was she doing this far away for Christmas Eve?'

'They had called her because the guy who was supposed to play in our church had disappeared after a couple of rehearsals. That was all James Hilton could tell me - a last minute arrangement', said Mike.

'Looks like no one really knew her', Margaret added and John nodded in agreement.

'There's not much details, I am afraid', Sarah said. Tom did a quick search on social media and there was not much luck.

'We could drive out to the West Ham parish church after Boxing Day and talk to the parish priest. That is an option', John said.

A valid point, everyone thought. But that meant Mike would have to wait for a couple of more days. Christmas and Boxing Day were not the great time to go around visiting churches. Given the festive atmosphere everywhere, especially the churches, it was going to be difficult getting some personal time with the parish priests.

'Two more days then', thought Mike. That was going to be undoubtedly restless.

The next two days were immensely restless as Mike had imagined it would be. But the feeling in him was different. This was a feeling of knowing that he had found something he had lost. This was a feeling of fullness. He had had a lot of sleepless nights feeling restless and diving deep into the void. But this restlessness was different. Though still he didn't know where it was leading him, he looked forward to finding the girl.

Just before Tom started back home he asked Mike, *'Are you sure that this girl is real and not your imagination?'*

'Don't you worry Tommy, I have still not gone insane!', Mike laughed. And they both laughed together after a long time – a very long time indeed.

Part VIII – The Search

The 27th of December 2011 was a Tuesday but still a bank holiday because Christmas had fallen on a Sunday. So, the roads were not very crowded except around the shopping malls and high streets. The drive was otherwise not very taxing. Tom and Sarah had very much wanted to come because they wanted Mike to brighten up in Life. They still felt guilty that they had their own responsibilities in whatever that had happened. But John had asked them to enjoy the holiday.

John and Mike spent most of the time in silence with some occasional references to what had happened over the four years. But otherwise Mike had the one piece of music for company. The interlude kept playing in his mind. And so did the thoughts of the beautiful fingers of Christina playing with the strings.

The parish priest of West Ham was father Patrick and he was over seventy years. But he looked far too old than his age. He spoke very slowly and very softly. Mike liked his friendly nature. John told him about who they were and what had happened.

'So young man, you are after a girl', he started with a jovial tone.

'Yes, father Patrick'

'Have you met Christie before?', father Patrick asked.

'You mean Christina?'

'Yes, I was referring to Christina. We call her Christie'

'No father, I have not met her or talked to her. I have listened to her music', Mike said and for a second thought if he had said 'his' music instead of 'her'.

'She is a nice girl and a very good guitarist. She was the best guitarist we have had in this church', father Patrick continued.

'Thought as much', said Mike. He was curiously waiting for the time to ask where he could meet her before which father Patrick broke the news.

'It is sad that she is leaving us today. She is moving down closer to her place of work'

The smile on Mike's face vanished. *'This is not going to be easy'*, he thought.

'Today, did you say?'

'Yes, she should have already packed everything', the parish priest said.

'Where can I find her now?', Mike asked in a real hurry. The sudden urgency caught the old priest by surprise.

'Oh, she lives on the street opposite to the main entrance of the West Ham stadium. It is the white apartments in the far corner. She lived there as a paying guest in a house number... 32 I think'

Mike and John thanked the parish priest and started to their car. Mike was very much running and John had trouble catching up. They drove off in a hurry. When they reached closer to the street, they hit a traffic jam.

'Where did all the traffic come from?', Mike was frustrated. The cars were moving only an inch every minute.

'What in the world is going on?', Mike cursed.

Slowly, they crossed the Boolean pub and into the road towards the Upton park station. The West Ham football stadium was just about there. But Mike had no time to wait.

'I'd better run while you wade through the traffic', said Mike. John nodded.

Mike jogged as fast as he could and he found the street that the parish priest had told about. He was in a hurry that he almost bumped into a white van that was waiting to join the slow-moving queue. The van covered most of road into the street. Mike somehow squeezed into the gap and he walked quickly to the apartment.

As he was going to ring the doorbell of the house number 32, some weird instinct in him asked him to turn around. Just as he turned, the van had just turned from the street on to the main road. The traffic seemed to be moving slightly faster than before. Had Mike turned a few seconds earlier, his search could have ended there. He would have seen a bright silver guitar case kept at the back of the van. Mike would have known it was Christina's.

Finally, someone answered the bell at the house number 32. The owners were a soft-spoken couple who looked to be at least sixty years old. The girl, Christina, was staying there as a paying guest for the last couple of years. Unfortunately, she had just vacated the house. She had not left a forwarding address but had agreed to come there in a few weeks' time to collect any mails.

The couple were very patient and Mike liked them immediately. Michael explained why he was there and why he was searching Christina. They had a lot of good things to tell about the girl.

'She took care of us like her own parents', the old lady said.

Mike and John thanked them. When they were about to leave, the old man asked them to wait and went to his room. He brought out a printed cup. It looked like a souvenir from a company.

'Christina gave it to us last year. She is an intern in this company – the finance department, I think', he said.

'Oh, that is very helpful of you', said Mike with a big smile – at least another clue he thought.

When Michael stepped out of the apartment, the old lady caught his hand and said, *'I used to tell her that one day, a prince would appear out of the blue and take her world by storm. But I didn't know that the day would come so soon'*. And then, she winked. Michael stood there trying to understand what the old lady had said but something sparked in him.

John pulled out his mobile and checked the company on the Internet. And the home page of the site said that they were closed till the New Year.

'Well, looks like more waiting for you', he said. Mike became silent. Something in him had changed. The wait and excitement of finding Christina had a new meaning since they left the old couples' apartment.

He smiled back and said, *'Looks like it sure is'*. After they reached home, Tom got on the phone with Sarah.

'Did you say it was in Piccadilly Circus?', she asked.

'Yeah, the map says it's closer to the Victorian theatre', Tom said.

'You know what, I have been through all those streets many times but I don't remember seeing the name of this company anywhere around Piccadilly Circus' Sarah said.

'Would you be able to take Mike around the area during your lunch time?', Tom asked.

'Sure, that would not be a problem. When would that be?', she asked.

'Monday, the 2nd', Tom said and Sarah agreed.

Part IX - The Search... Continues

The 2nd of January 2012 was not as bright a day Mike expected it to be. The New Year Day had just come and gone just like any other day. Mike had not even noticed it go by. The four days since he had come back from the West Ham parish sailed at a snail's pace. He was excited as he was worried. He was normal as he was abnormal. Something didn't feel so well but at the same time things felt very different.

'Mike, are you sure you can take the tube into London?', Sarah asked over the phone. After a few minutes, everyone had asked the same question. Since the incident four years back,

Mike had reached the doors of the London Underground train only once. But it was not a memorable outing. The thoughts of the incident struck like lightning and he passed out. The enquiries made by everyone seemed reasonable but seemed to make him nervous.

The national rail from Reading to London Paddington seemed fine but it was the ride on the Bakerloo line that made him nervous. He was palpitating and sweating during the entire journey. He was almost a nervous wreck when he got out. He had continuous visions of the incident but at the end of it, he had managed pretty well. It seemed to be some kind of an achievement.

He walked along with the crowd out of the train and towards the escalators. The London Underground stations had a lot of slots for musicians to play and that day someone was playing the guitar and he was brilliant. Mike wanted to stop for a minute and listen to the guy play *'Newton Faulkner's "Gone in the morning"'*. But he knew Sarah was waiting outside the station for him.

The song was one of his favourites in the contemporary list and the guitarist was making it sound even better. His eyes were on the guitar and how the fingers were playing with the strings. It was quite a sight. The escalators at the Piccadilly Circus station were one of the longest and number of stairs in operation at a given time was far higher than a lot of other stations. Many people felt dizzy just by looking down from the top. Mike was concentrating on the guitarist as he went up the escalator.

Just about the same time he stepped on to the escalator going up, a girl carrying a silver guitar case stepped on the escalator in the other direction. She had a serpent tattoo on her hand – just like his. Had Mike not concentrated on the guitarist but looked up, he would have seen the guitar case but that, of course, did not happen.

Just a few seconds before Mike turned around in her direction, the girl took the guitar case off her shoulders and placed it on the stairs of the escalator and it could not be seen from the other side. Mike saw the girl but he did not know who it was.

Sarah helped Mike go around the Piccadilly circus streets. She had worked in a theatre there before and knew the places quite well. After a bit of a struggle, they found the office they were looking for. When they reached the reception, what they got was dejecting news.

'Christie completed her internship here before the Christmas break. She has a new job about which we know no further details', the receptionist said.

'Somebody should have known something', pressed Mike.

'Sorry sir, we cannot help you any further', was the stern reply. *'It would be a breach to give any personal details of current or previous employees.'*

Mike felt totally devastated. This seemed to be only positive lead he had but it was a dead end. They didn't have much of an option but to leave. Mike did not utter a word on the way back to the office elevator. Sarah tried to find the right words but it did not help.

'Are you here to see Christie?', a man asked from behind.

Mike was startled and he nodded very quickly. It was an old man in his late fifties who seemed to be an attendant in the office.

'Well, she works here no more. But, she goes to the church in Holborn every Monday afternoon. You should be able to see her there in about... Well, now'

Mike was excited again. He felt exhilarated by the news and almost hugged the man. He thanked him almost a million times and ran down the stairs not wanting to wait for the elevator. Sarah had a difficult time adjusting to the sudden rush of energy and could not catch her breath.

'Slow down, Mikey', she kept saying while chasing Mike all the way to the train station.

The station was jam packed with people and the escalators were full of people standing in two lines. Sarah was thankful for the crowd because she could finally catch up with Michael.

'Slow down, dude', she always pleaded.

'Sorry...', Mike said apologetically.

'Tell me something...', she hesitated.

'What?', he asked.

'Have you fallen in love with this girl who you have even not met before?', she asked out of the blue.

Mike did not know. And that was his answer too. The feeling in him was inexplicable – truly inexplicable. He never had known how to put things into words and this was far too complicated for him.

'I don't know Sarah. I don't think I can explain it. But...', he didn't know what to say.

'But what...?'

'But... I think she will complete me', he said. *'I know I haven't even seen her. But I can feel it. She seems to be everything I have always been. And, she, I think, will be everything I can never be. She will be the music in me',* he finished. Sarah almost choked. She was taken aback by how beautifully Mike had put it.

'I don't know what they call it from where you come from', and with joy she screamed, *'But from where I come from, they call it Love Mr. Harris!'*

The Piccadilly line train towards Uxbridge was not so crowded compared to the previous train ride. Sarah and Mike got down at Holborn and started walking towards the exit. Just as he crossed a vestibule of the train, something struck him. He realised it only after he had walked a few more steps.

What he had seen was a girl standing near the door holding the bar with her right hand. The tattoo had caught his attention – the serpent tattoo and by her side was the silver guitar case. It was the girl he was searching for the last few days. The girl he had crossed was Christina Sahayaraj.

Michael was caught off guard with the sudden development in the situation. He had not expected to see her. He was hyper excited. But as fate would have it, doors of the train closed when he turned and walked towards her.

'Oh Damn!', he said and the train started moving.

He started running with the train, trying to garner the girl's attention in the train and at the same time trying to avoid bumping into anyone on the platform. But she was facing the other direction and all he could see was her hand, the tattoo and the guitar case. The train gathered speed and he could not catch up with it.

Sarah came running behind him and almost slammed into him, *'What in the world is wrong with you?'*

'It's the girl. Christina!'

'What? How did you know?', she asked.

'I saw her tattoo. The serpent tattoo! It was Christina!', he said with sureness in his voice. He pointed to the tattoo on his hand saying it was the same tattoo.

'Oh God, we missed her by a whisker!', she said.

'Damn, yeah!', he responded trying to bring his breathing down. The next Piccadilly line train was in eight minutes said the electronic board.

'She could be anywhere in that time', he cursed. They sat on the benches till they calmed down but Michael's mind was just racing.

'How did I not see her a few seconds before?', he kept asking himself. He did not have an answer. Michael was silent throughout their journey back to Reading. He was sad that he had not had a chance to meet the girl and even worse, when the opportunity came close, he could not acknowledge it appropriately. As fate had it written, he had crossed her more than one time and had not seen her in any of the occasions.

'Yeah, he says he saw her but I am not sure honey', Sarah was on the phone with Tom. She handed over the phone to Mike. Tom tried to console him but could not. Michael was still dejected and tired after the day.

'Ok, meet you at the Irish pub', Tom said finally.

'I don't think it's a good time to go to the pub, Tommy', he replied.

'Ah, give it a rest, will you? It would be a change of scene and you would feel better', he said.

'Well...', started Mike but Tom did not let him finish.

'Martin wants to see you too', said Tom.

Martin Ceara was the manager at the Irish bar. He had been friends with Mike and Tom for a good two decades. And it had been a long time since Mike had seen him.

Sarah patted his shoulders and said in a reassuring voice, *'Don't you worry. We will find her'*

Part X - The Accident

It was almost six pm when they reached Reading. It was not a scene they expected to see outside the station. The commotion was quite out of the ordinary in a relatively less busy station like Reading. The line of police vehicles with the blue lights flashing, the ambulance ready to steer away and the sound of the siren freaked everyone out.

'What in the world is going on?', Sarah asked when they stepped out.

'I don't know, looks like some kind of an accident', said Mike. They quickly walked to the crowd that had gathered around the area.

'What happened?', they asked to a group of young chaps.

'A lady was run down by the Rover', one of them said pointing to a black Land Rover.

'Is she alright?', Sarah probed.

'We don't know. But it looked pretty serious to me'

'A lady?', asked Sarah.

'Yeah, the lady was someone from the Church choir. I heard it from the guy who identified her when the ambulance came'

This sent a shudder through Mike's brain. His head was spinning and he felt his pulse to be unbearably high. His vision was blurred and he was almost going to black out.

'Was it Christina?', he gasped. Tom had walked down from the bar. Before anyone could grasp the situation, Mike dashed towards the ambulance cutting through the file of police officers at the scene. He was stopped by the police and was not allowed to cross the barricades. Just as he was pleading with the officers to let him through to see the lady, Tom and Sarah rushed to the spot and pulled him back.

'What is wrong with you, Mike?', shouted Tom. *'This madness ends right now!'*

'It could be Christina!', Mike blurted.

'What? Who?!'

'It could be Christina who is in that ambulance!'.

'What are you talking about?', Sarah asked.

'Mikey, the lady who was hit by the car cannot be Christina. At least not your Christina!', continued Tom.

'What do you mean? How do you know?'

'The lady was fifty years old. She was a singer in the church not a guitarist. That's what I mean and that's how I know! God... Damn... it...!!', shrieked Tom.

'And this lady is going to be fine, I hear. She fainted in shock and has a broken wrist— nothing critical', he said at a stretch and walked towards the bar. Mike stood there and after almost a heart attack he breathed a sigh of relief. He knew for himself that he had acted very weird in the last few minutes.

'Come on Mike', Sarah pulled him along to the bar.

Martin was genuinely happy to see Mike after all the years, *'Wow, that is really you! Mike, how are you?'*, he said with a contagious enthusiasm.

He took them to their usual slot at the far quiet corner. Mike felt very happy and relaxed on seeing his old friend. Martin brought Tom and Sarah with their usual beer and cider.

He then turned to Mike and said, *'Well, let me see if I remember it right - a cup of tea with one shot of skimmed milk, half a shot of cream and two spoons of sugar - brown and a hint of cinnamon. Right?'*

Mike smiled and said, *'Absolutely!'*

'I run an Irish bar and I could serve any drink you name but you would be the only person on earth who would settle for a prescription based tea', Martin smiled as he brought Mike his cup of tea.

'A cup of tea in the Irish Pub', smiled Sarah. *'Interesting choice!'*

Michael's thoughts slowly went back to Christina. He was so close to meeting her but he could not. He really wanted to meet her. His feelings for her grew every single minute.

'Sarah was right', he told himself. *'This must be love!'*.

The bar was slowly becoming crowded. A group of four girls had just sat down diagonal to Mike's slot. Martin took their orders on his way to see Mike and Tom.

'That was weird', Martin said.

'What was weird?', Tom asked.

'You know what the girl there ordered?', asked Martin still looking at his order sheet.

'What?', Sarah asked curiously.

'Déjà vu', said Martin *'a cup of tea with one shot of skimmed milk, half a shot of cream, two spoons of sugar – brown and a hint of cinnamon'*

'Who would have thought there were two of you?', Martin winked as he walked back.

All the three blinked to see if he was joking. Mike had an odd feeling in his chest and turned around to see who it was. Just as he turned, one of the girls moved a silver guitar case to the side to sit comfortably. Then she took of her gloves to reveal a beautiful serpent tattoo. It was her. *It was Christina Sahayaraj.*

Mike turned back to Tom and Sarah to check if he was dreaming. They understood that it was her. He had been running to the ends of the city in search of her and she lands right in front of him – What were the odds? He could not believe his eyes.

It looked, sounded and felt completely surreal. It was just like a dream. The girl of his life was sitting just a few feet away. This girl was going to be every bit of the lost music in his life. She was going to complete him in every way. She was the music of his life. His feet were not on the ground. *Everything except Christina was just a blur. She was beautiful. She was as beautiful as his music.*

Unsure of what to do and what to say, he took a step forward towards her. With every unsure step he took towards her, the rate of heartbeat leaped higher. He was becoming more and more nervous. Sarah and Tom watched in excitement. Tom was already calling his parents' numbers. The excitement caught up with Martin too, though he did not have a clue of what was happening.

Every single step of Mike towards Christina seemed to take an era. He slowly and steadily said, *'Christina?'*.

She was startled for a second but her eyes said *'Yes?'*

He looked calmly into her vibrant blue eyes and lent his hand to introduce himself, *'I am Michael Harris'*.

The noise in the bar subdued and the interlude played loud in his mind. It was not his interlude. It was not hers. It was now theirs – *Their interlude*. He hoped she would understand that she was the one. He hoped she would understand that she was his music and his love. He hoped she would understand that she would make his life complete.

At that moment, to Michael Harris, **Hope... Was... Everything...**

See you tomorrow, gorgeous

The weird feeling in her mind had not subdued even a little bit in the last few weeks. It was getting stronger as the days went by. The thoughts were making her nervous and kept recurring quite a few times a day.

'I am definitely being followed' she thought strongly.

She was just a simpleton going through life paycheck to paycheck. It was beyond any valid explanation why someone would take an interest in her, let alone follow her for days together.

For some inexplicable reason, the feeling was intense that evening. She was unable to shake it off. As she sat in the train waiting for it to move, she was feeling more and more weird. The train operator had just announced that there were going to be minor delays due to adverse weather conditions.

'Just a little fog!', she let out an exasperated sigh when she heard the usual 'Adverse weather conditions' being mentioned for the millionth time that evening.

She slowly looked around her as the train made a slow and steady move forward. The carriage was half-empty and most of the seats behind her were unoccupied. A half-asleep man, an old couple and two women dressed too brightly for the evening were the only passengers in sight.

'You are just being paranoid for no reason!', her boyfriend had told her followed by an *'It's all going to be fine'* when she had mentioned the sense of fear that had been eating her mind. Apparently his usually motivating line *'Trust your instincts, babe!'* was obsolete in the given instance. *'Men!'* was the only reaction that came to mind whenever she thought about it.

'Maybe it is the lack of sleep that's causing me all the troubling thoughts', she gave herself a self-diagnosis. She had not slept well for a good few days. She was not sure if this paranoia was the cause of the sleepless nights or if it was the other way around.

Not being able to focus on anything and the anxiety slowly getting the better of it, she stood up from her seat and walked to the door. The fog had reduced the visibility so much that even the lights that lined the sides of the tracks were barely visible. But there was a serene feeling looking into the emptiness of the fog. Her stop was just a few minutes away but the train was slowing down once every couple of minutes to increase her frustration.

'Fucking delays!', she cursed louder than she had intended to. The old lady in the carriage turned to give her a shake of the head noting it was not good to swear in public. She could not give anything any damn attention for that moment.

As the train slowly crawled into the platform, she checked her reflection on the doors. She ran her fingers through her silky blonde hair to set it to perfection and looked at the reflection of her blue eyes for a good few seconds. The train doors opened and she wasted no time. The fog had created a deeply intense eeriness in the station. On a given day, she thought, a million people got down with her at the station but it was far quieter that evening.

'Where is everybody?', she asked herself. She felt they should be the lucky ones that opted to work from home citing the same 'adverse weather conditions'. She wondered what that felt like - to work from home.

As she usually did, she plugged the headphones into her phone to shut herself out of the annoying world around her as she walked home. The fog made it difficult to see even a few feet around. She looked around her and to the far end of the platform before she took the flight of stairs to the station exit. All she could see were some shadows floating here and there.

She could not hear any music as she stepped out onto the platform. She looked at her phone which for some reason had decided to die on her. She tried to switch it on a few times with no luck. It was foggy enough to avoid any distractions, she thought. She needed all of her senses to function to their fullest to wade through the blinding fog.

She heard footsteps behind her and before she could realise, a man ran past her almost pushing her aside. The little consolation of getting home after a tiring day at work dissipated without a hint. A sense of fear raced through her nerves as a strong cold wind brushed her neck and sent a literal chill down her spine. The man ran up to a car parked on the other side of the road.

She quickened her steps and waded through the few lights of other cars waiting outside the station to pick up other passengers. The yellow and red lights of the cars and vans painted glowing waves in the fog. They slightly reminded her of the Northern Lights in Greenland only less beautiful and more ghastly.

She crossed the main road and turned right to the stretch that had the century-old church at its far end. She kept walking throwing a quick glance behind her once in a while to ensure no one was following her or planning to mug her when there was a chance. She wondered if the martial arts classes she had taken with a few of her female colleagues would be of even a teeny tiny help.

She was a bit late to realise it but when she did, she slowed down her steps. There were about three street lamps that were malfunctioning at that minute. She was sure that they were working when she turned onto the street. It was pitch dark and she was not sure if she could just cross the darkness in one quick walk or if she should just run like a crazy person.

Her evening had been weird enough that her heart rate was through the roof. She was worried crazy. She looked back one more time and decided to just keep walking. A good few steps into the darkness, something in her told her to stop. She did not know why or what but she stopped.

Then, she heard it.

She heard a shallow... coarse... breathing... Too coarse to be anything human. Then as if their break was over, the street lights came on.

It took her a good few seconds for her mind to register what was standing in front of her in the fog. It was a dog, that was for sure but not the ones that she would have wanted to play with or tried to cuddle when she had a chance. If she had known better, she would have known it was a Doberman Pinscher. It belonged to one of the varieties which would hurt the enemy or prey before they even made a move. It was enormous and the mere sight of which would send shivers through the bravest of men.

She could see the breath of the dog like a dragon letting out smoke. The dog looked angry and every passing second made it look even more monstrous than it actually was. She could see the teeth glittering in the low light. Its eyes glistened and even through the fog she knew they were looking straight at her. A cold sweat appeared on her forehead and her heart was almost up in her throat. She could not breathe and her knees were giving up in the pressure of the moment.

The dog took a few quiet steps towards her. She did not know if she had to do anything - more importantly whether she would be able to do anything. She took a step back matching the animals every step towards her. The animal let out a loud growl which felt more like a lion than a dog. She took it as an order from the stronger creature to stop moving. She stood still.

The moment was intense. She stood frozen still and the animal held its ground. Its breathing intensified. She felt the stare to be sharper than before. She decided that she was going to make a run for it - whatever happened, she was going to run.

Just as she decided to run, there was a low but clear owl-whistle. She turned to the direction where the sound had come from and so did the big unfriendly dog.

Then came a similarly low but double owl-whistle as if it was a signal. The animal immediately let its guard down and walked like a little kid into the darkness.

She stood there in fear, nothing but absolute fear. One moment she had thought she was going to be attacked by the ferocious dog and the next minute there was nothing. The fear of the animal was one thing but it was more frightening that there was someone in the darkness. She kept staring into the darkness trying to make out anything resembling a person.

'Sorry!', said a voice from the distance. The sudden voice startled her even more. All she could see was the grim outline of the old church. In the fog, the church looked more ungodly than it actually was in reality. She walked away from the spot quietly in confusion and fear.

'Should be the parish priest's dog', she thought, remembering an age-old conversation with one of the parishioners. Slowly a sense of relief took over her. The last half a kilometer of her walk was going to be between barricades that had been put up for road works that seemed to have been going on for years. She quickly checked if there was anything remotely looking like a dog following her.

The eerie quietness settled down again and there were no vehicles on the road nearby. She kept walking and turned into the high street to take a shortcut home. No one in their right minds took the high streets in the dark. Her only thought of reaching home faster made her do so. Just as she took a few steps into the dark alley through the high street, she realised it was a mistake. Two teenage kids on their BMX bikes wearing dark hoodies raced towards her.

They freaked her out as she braced herself to be hit by one or both of the bikes. They narrowly missed her as if on purpose and sped away as quickly as they had appeared. They let out a huge laugh as they raced away and the echo in the alley was unbearable.

'Fucking bastards!', she shouted and tears came running down her cheeks. They smudged her mascara and flowed in

two long black streaks. Too many things had happened in one evening that she just could not help but cry. She was too frightened to move. She took off her high heeled shoes and decided to run home. She kept running and was in no mood to stop for anything. Tears kept coming as if everything that had bundled up in her mind as stress was flowing out. She did not even slow down till she reached her apartment entrance.

There was a car standing at ten meters from the entrance of her flats. The engine was still running. The bright red light of the rear lamp threw a ghostly blanket in the foggy evening. She turned around for, what she hoped was, the last time that evening and touched the key fob for the door to open. The light on the door did not turn green and the door did not open. She tried again and again in vain.

She let out a sigh and let out an exasperated *'Seriously?'*.

She ruffled into her bag that contained a million and one items to get the key that she was looking for. A good few seconds' search was finally fruitful. As she pulled out the key from her bag, she saw a shadow come into her peripheral view. A pang fear hit her like a log. A shiver ran violently from head to toe. Whoever it was, the person was walking straight to her. She realized that she had crossed a threshold of fear that evening and she was going to physically fall down in a second.

The person came nearer and nearer and finally she saw a hand appear. She could not find her voice and not a speck of sound came from her dry throat. Too scared to do anything, she just gave up. She left everything to fate - whatever that was supposed to happen was indeed going to happen. She waited... waited... and waited.

The person crossed her without even hesitating and unlocked the door and no harm was done to her. She slowly turned to look at who it was. It was a lady from her apartment carrying a baby on her back who had just opened the door for her. A sense of overwhelming relief rushed through her. She looked at the lady and the baby without even blinking. The baby's earth green eyes had a mesmerizing effect that brought a sense of serenity.

'Thank you!' she managed to whisper to the lady as they went in separate ways towards their respective flats. The baby turned to see her again and smiled.

She was exhausted when she entered her apartment and she dropped half dead onto her couch. She had no energy to even move a muscle. The intense evening had drained her physically and psychologically. She did not even think if any of her fears were real or the whole evening was just one big fucking coincidence.

'You are just being paranoid', she reminded herself of her boyfriend's words.

'Maybe it's just the lack of sleep', she told herself. The heavy door and strong four walls around her gave her a sense of safety and her mind seemed to work more pragmatically. She took off her clothes and she stepped into a hot shower. As the hot water cleansed her body, her mind cleared itself of all the fear and anxiety. A sense of calm returned. She messaged her boss that she was unwell and won't be at work for a couple of days, followed up with a couple of shots of whiskey and sank into her bed.

Just about the time she got into a deep slumber and started feeling safer, a man she did not know, a man she had never met eye to eye, finished looking at the pictures he had taken of her that foggy evening. He had followed her closely for a good few days.

'She sure looks beautiful when her eyes are wide open with fear', he told himself satisfied with the pictures he had managed to click on an awfully foggy day. He looked at the pictures of her one last time before packing away his gear.

He had nothing planned for her - not yet at least. He was not sure what he was going to do with her. The decision with other women had been simple and straightforward. But there was something about her blue eyes that did not allow him to make a quick final decision.

He threw his backpack over his shoulder and patted the Doberman Pinscher standing next to him. He took a deep breath of the cold foggy air and a smile appeared on his face after a deeply satisfying evening.

*'**See you tomorrow, gorgeous**'* he said as he disappeared slowly into the foggy night.

The twenty-seven seconds...

He had been a creature of habit. Every single thing had to be done in precisely the way he wanted and at the exact time he wanted. He hated people and people hated him. He went on with his life without an even a hint of regard for anyone or anything. He did the same things every single day like a droid, only he was not one. Life was more like clockwork. Maybe, it was exactly *'clockwork'*

He woke up every day at the same time, did the same number of minutes on the cross trainer, spent the same amount of time in the shower, ate the same wheatgerm bread toast with crunchy peanut butter for breakfast, left home at the same time, took the same train and almost did the same kind of work every single day - Every day for the past 2 years.

Einstein defined *'Insanity'* as *'Doing the same thing over and over again and expecting different results'*.

'I am not insane by that definition. I don't expect different results', he told himself many times.

He lived. No, he existed. He did not know why he had become that way and did not question it. He just went on with his life. Existed. He was neither happy nor sad. 'I just tag along' was his simple explanation even though no one asked him for one. He did not have any friends, he was not on social media, he did not know many people at work - No emotional connection whatsoever. And before those two years - it all just a blur for him. Nothing significant had happened to be remembered for... almost forever.

How someone like him existed could need work of famous mathematicians or statisticians to figure out. But he lived. He existed like an age old mechanical watch on a museum wall.

Just... Existed...

When he went to sleep on that Wednesday, he had no idea that everything was going to be put to a test.

It all looked normal when he woke up at his usual time. He did his usual cross training followed by the shower. Even the sandwich was fine almost until the last bite. Whether the toast was a bit extra heated or if the peanut butter was not of the usual quality, he did not know. But it had melted a bit more than usual and a very small little drop of the melted peanut butter dripped onto his tie.

'For fuck sake!' he said out loud. His words echoed in his tiny little apartment. It was one of the first words that were spoken in that little space and the words resonated in shock. He looked at his watch and let out a sigh. He knew he had a bit of time with the coffee which he could take in his travel mug. He quickly rushed to the sink to scrub away the bit of peanut butter off of his tie.

'Ah!', he said out loud. He had made it worse; the tough stain would just not go. He decided to change his tie and rush. Whether it was the sudden change in pattern or just the rush of doing it, he felt weird. His heart was beating faster and his hands were shivering slightly - clear symptoms of the Obsessive Compulsive Disorder that he was quite sure he had. He took a deep breath, changed his tie and walked into the kitchen. He poured the strong black coffee into the travel mug that was on the shelf unused for quite a while. He rushed out of the house with coffee in one hand and his bag in the other.

There was a weird attachment that he had with that particular travel mug. Though calling it his favorite would be stretching it a bit too far. That was the first little thing he bought when he got his first teeny tiny paycheck. It felt that it was a whole millennium old but it had come in handy in unusual situations like that he faced that very day.

He glanced at his watch and was slightly convinced that he was back on track. Whether it was a psychological problem or whether it was an acute case of OCD, he did not care. It was his life and he was going to live it his way.

When he came out of his apartment building and onto the pavement of the main road, he knew it was going to take him twelve minutes to reach the station. He started walking like a machine without even thinking much. It was a slight uphill walk half the way and then downhill till the station. So he could not see anything on the side below the line of view. The December sun was just shining bright into his eyes. It was a typical winter morning. The dew, the intense chillness in the air, the freshness, it was all there. But he didn't notice anything - maybe he resisted noticing them.

The road looked void of people or traffic. It was quite usual for him not to come face to face with anyone most days. Just when everything looked normal and void, he saw someone run uphill from the other side, probably a morning runner. A few seconds later as the person came running closer, he noticed it was a girl. Her posture, clothes, and the strides that she took made her look like a pro. She had just come uphill and she was picking up speed in his direction. The sun was behind her but her face was clear from the light reflected from the surroundings.

The bright orange sunlight, the freshness of the winter morning, the dew on the grass and leaves - they all clicked in his mind for the first time in a long time. Was it the presence of the girl or was it something else that stirred a change in him, he was not sure. She was gathering speed and was running towards him. She looked beautiful.

Without his knowledge, his legs slowed down. Every step she took made his heart skip a few beats. The moment was beautiful. He had never realised a moment in life could resonate with such beauty. And before he came back to his senses, she was just a couple of seconds away.

What he failed to realise in that moment was that he was right in her path blocking her way. His deep brown eyes met her cool blue eyes for a moment and before he knew it, she jumped off the pavement shouting *'Watch out!'*. But she did not avoid contact with him. She brushed his arm and at the speed she was running and his momentary lapse in concentration the mug flipped in his hand and the strong black coffee splattered all over him.

'Watch out you fucking Weirdo!', she shouted as she continued running sparing not even a moment.

Her words hung in the cold air like a burst of sprayed hot water. For a few seconds, it did not register in his mind. But when it did, his face turned extremely red with anger. All for letting his defenses down for just a good few seconds. He looked again in the direction the girl had run. But she was nowhere to be seen.

He was so angry that, even in that intense cold of a winter morning, his skin was burning. He did not know what to do and through his clenched teeth he angrily moaned, *'That stupid bitch!'*

He shouted those words over and over for a good few times and then looked at his watch.

He was late by a good four minutes and twenty seconds. His jacket was all wet with the spilled coffee. There would be about one or two gulps of coffee left in the mug, he thought. He checked if the mug was closed tight and decided to make a run to the station.

He gained control over his running but it was just too much for him. Within a minute of running, he realised it was an entirely different ball game. However, fit he had thought he was, he knew it was all a waste when it came to running. He huffed and puffed slowing every minute of running. He cursed the girl every chance he had for putting him through this.

It was because of her he was late, he thought. But it was deep rooted in him that she had insulted him. That hurt him more. She had called him a weirdo. However true that could or could not be, the word insulted him.

'How dare she?!', he thought.

He could see he was regaining lost time. He was nearing the station and it was as busy as it always was. His old digital watch said he was behind by a minute. He kept running as he got to the ticket gates. The clock on the platform that he religiously trusted showed he was twenty-seven seconds late. He could see the train already in the distance.

He ran up the flight of stairs to get to the right platform which, unfortunately, was the farthest. The train was already pulling into the platform. The footbridge was fairly long and he did not want to lose any time by slowing down. He was quite sure that he could catch the train and then things would just return to normal.

His body was almost going to give up. His nerves were wrecking. Though the sign on the bridge clearly said 'DO NOT RUN', he decided to ignore it. He would have taken about fourteen steps on the bridge when he saw it. He noticed a small bag at the far end of the platform. In the moment of rush, he decided to ignore that as well.

He continued to run and he could see that the doors of the train had just opened and a stream of passengers rushed out.

And then, it happened.

The bomb in the unattended little bag that he decided to ignore, went off with the loudest noise he could have ever imagined. The explosion was blindingly bright.

The explosion was very vivid in that moment. Every detail of it was precisely clear to him. The flames tearing open the bag and expanding and growing in rage. He could see the explosion growing in volume in front of him and approaching him like a devil. The glass around him shattered. The brick and mortar flew up in pieces everywhere. Everything appeared in a clear minute detail till a mighty force hit him like a heavy truck. The force threw him a good few feet into the far wall.

The moment he crashed into the wall, a searing pain rushed through every inch of his body. As if his body was reacting to the pain, the world went dark.

What happened in the next few hours were just sporadic flashes of memories to him as he went in and out of consciousness. There was a continuous pounding in his head and his ears were ringing. The blast and the smoke... The debris... People running towards him... The sound of sirens... The commotion... The police... and finally the ambulance... A few seconds after the paramedics sent drugs down his veins, a sense of peace enveloped him.

It was no less than twenty-seven hours later when he opened his eyes again. The throbbing in his head had not gone away and there were severe aches in a million places across his body. His vision ebbed a good few times before things came into focus.

'Looks like someone is finally awake', said a lady with a thick accent. He could not move his head or turn his neck but he understood that it was the nurse who was talking to him. The effects of the sedatives and painkillers were still prevalent. The nurse came into his view and told him with a confident smile, *'You are one lucky guy, you know that?!'*.

A lot of doctors came to see him that afternoon to explain various things to him. The psychologist was the most interesting of the lot trying to explain Post Traumatic Stress Disorder to him. The discussion made him feel weird as he was not sure if the 'stressful event' was his few years of life before the blast or if it was to with life after the blast.

It took him four complete days to feel close to normal again. There were bruises and minor injuries from the blast but there were not going to be any permanent physical damages. He was scheduled for a few follow-up appointments with the physiotherapist and psychologists in the next few weeks and months.

Having been the only person, but still a very lucky one at that, to be physically impacted by the blast made him a mini-celebrity. There were repeated news shows and articles in the paper about the incident and he was mentioned and talked about in almost all of them. He had stopped following the news on any kind of media. He had a strong belief that they focused on a specific set of events to mainly keep something hidden from the world's view. The news was not sacred anymore, in his strong opinion.

Quite a few things had happened in his personal life too. His mother and father had been to see him at the hospital. He was quite sure his father had not been bald the last time he had seen him. His wife, technically his ex-wife, had been on the phone quite a few times. And his son, who hated him just enough to not talk to him, had promised to come and visit him in a few days. Though he knew that these were temporary reactions, he just let things be. Somewhere in the corner of his heart and mind he felt this to be a new start for him. It was indeed a life changing event.

As he waited for his belongings to be brought to him, his thoughts went back to the day of the event. He knew that the little incident involving the girl had everything to do with how it had all turned out. If they had not crossed each other's' path, he knew very well that he could have been blown to pieces that day. The more he thought about her, the more he wanted to see her again.

When he was handed his belongings, he checked everything to be in order except for the severe stains on his packed clothes. Given that he was lucky enough to have been unscathed by an incident of that magnitude, he didn't worry about the condition of his belongings - whether it was the coffee that was spilled or if it was the dirt from the blast and the debris, he did not care. He felt a little sad to have not seen his coffee mug in the belongings - should have shattered and now been buried in a heap of rubbish, he thought.

The final moments at the hospital were a bit dramatic. There were news crews waiting for him outside the hospital, he was visited by a few heads of politics and the social media had gone haywire with his pictures and articles about him. He had to wade through a fair number of people to get to the taxi waiting for him. The taxi driver did not accept any money for the ride.

All through the ride home, his thoughts kept going back to the girl. Her face was very clear in his memories. He could feel a sudden rush of excitement when he thought of the moment when his eyes met her blue eyes. The calmness of her face up until the moment when he called him a weirdo was intriguing. The more and more people said, *'you are lucky to be alive'*, the more indebted he felt to her. He would have been dead if she had not crossed his path, he firmly believed.

He walked slowly from the cab to his apartment. He knew that in a few days' time, his life would slowly fall into the same pit it was before. How much ever he tried to think of this as a fresh start, he could not push the loneliness out of his mind. He had a few media interviews agreed in the coming days but he was not sure if he had to mention the girl to them. Maybe that would help him meet her again, he thought. Maybe meeting her again would help him take his new lease of life forward. The more he thought of the chances, the more he was anxious to find her.

Her face, the serene blue eyes, the moment of that cold beautiful morning, all brought a smile to his face. A smile! *'How long had that been since he smiled?!'* he asked himself.

His apartment looked undisturbed during his time at the hospital. Everything was just as he had left them. He would have to clear his refrigerator and his recycle bin. He settled on his couch to take a few deep breaths and relish his time being alive. He recollected that last time he had left his house.

The tie... the peanut butter... the coffee... the mug... the events all came back one by one. The line of thoughts ended with the girl.

Who was she? Was she just someone who he had accidently met? Or was she more than that?

'Maybe an angel', he thought.

Just as he walked towards the kitchen, the thoughts of the girl brought another smile to his lips. But before it became a fully satisfied smile, he saw something.

The cold black coffee from that cold morning was still on the table.

His favorite mug still sat untouched for ages on the shelf.

Those beautiful blue eyes...

Up until that point it was just another ordinary day in the Mercy Hospital in Cork. It all changed when the speeding ambulance rushed in. The patient was covered in blood but was, with considerable difficulty, still breathing. He had three bullet wounds and had lost a lot of blood. He was in and out of consciousness for a good few minutes.

'Don't you fucking die, you son of a bitch!', someone was screaming at him but he could not see who it was. His vision was ebbing to every beat of his heart.

'You will be fine! You will be fine!', someone else was saying.

It all went quiet all of sudden. He could not hear anything except for his breath. And once in a while he felt his heartbeat sending a shudder through his head. He was not scared of the severe stillness that the world around him had come to. His eyes fought with all the willpower to stay open. His eyes kept searching though – searching to see those beautiful blue eyes one last time.

Then... he flatlined.

Part I: Ireland

A sudden jolt woke him up from his dream. It had turned turbulent all of a sudden and the flight was trying get out of the way. It took him more than a few minutes to realise where he was. He shook his head to gather his thought.

'Ah, the flight to Dublin!', it came back to him.

He had taken the 06:45 flight out of London Heathrow. He was extremely tired, thanks to a hectic week. To add to all the tiredness, he had a good few hours' drive to Cork ahead of him after landing in Dublin.

He had been in Ireland once before during what were the most beautiful days of his life. He had driven around Ireland with Rachel by his side. He saw two of God's beautiful creations together at the same place – Rachel and the beauty of Ireland. Though years had gone by, his friends still said the places remained as lovely as ever.

'I am Andy – Andrew Reynolds', he said as he lent out his hand to offer a handshake to the old lady sitting next to him. It had been just ten minutes since he had woken up from his sleep but she had already told him the story of her entire life.

'Oh boy, I should have stayed silent', he thought.

'So, what do you do for a living?', she asked which he didn't really want to explain to the lady but she insisted.

'Well, I actually run a small private service. We spend time... Well, how to put it... Let's say, I track people – A Finder'.

'Oh, a private detective?', she asked.

'No. Not like that'

'Or a spy, espionage something like that eh?', she sounded like someone who watched a lot of movies.

'I find long lost people and bring them back to their families or loved ones. We don't do it as a business per se. It's more of a service to people who come to us asking for help.', Andy said.

The lady immediately started sobbing, *'That is so nice of you!'*

'Thanks!'

'You remind me of my husband', she said. *'He liked to help people as well. It's been five years since he passed away and I miss him dearly'*

After she dozed off, Andy sat there thinking how things usually turned up when he tried to track down people. His little team would track the digital footprints that people leave. But that got them only to a certain level. That was usually followed by ground work identifying contacts and people to help in the area. Then came the slightly difficult step when Andy got there in person to investigate and find the person. The most difficult of the entire search was when they found the person – the confrontation. In most cases, it ended well – Most cases.

He had recently tracked down a boy who had left home six years back after an intense quarrel with his father. His father, who looked like a stubborn man, sank to his knees when he saw his son again. That moment was inexplicable. Or the stepmother in different case – she had married a much older man whose daughter never got along well with her. When the daughter had left the house to join a cult of sorts, the lady was quite happy but the guilt of such a horrible thing would not let her be. It took Andy and his little team about a year and half to locate her. After a bad start, it was now a one happy family.

But sometimes, it all went up in flames. About two weeks ago, he had helped a middle-aged couple from the south of England to find their daughter who had disappeared with her boyfriend eight years ago. The situation was the most complicated Andy had ever seen. He tried his best to get the girl safely back to her parents but he had to face a whole bunch of things – Gangs, drugs, prostitution, and pimps. It got uglier and uglier. He ended up getting the police involved and unknowingly busted a whole drug operation. The girl was now safe with her parents but Andrew Reynolds would have been history if he did not make the right move at the right time in that case.

He remembered those moments vividly. He was caught by the gang and had a gun pressed against his head. The drug lord's face had a huge scar and tattoos covering his entire arm. The police had come bursting through the door right at that very last second when he was about to pull the trigger. From the look in the man's eyes when he was arrested, Andy knew it was not even close to being over.

It was about 08:00 in the morning when the flight landed and Andy got the car he had hired in less than twenty minutes. He decided to take the N11 instead of the short M7/M8 route just for one reason – The beauty of Ireland. The beautiful drive from Dublin to Cork was worth the longer drive. It was nothing short of stunning. He wondered how people could just drive by the scenic routes every day without the temptation to stop and immerse themselves in God's lovely painting. He just wished he could park the car on the road and just get lost in the woods.

Andy took a slight diversion to Abbeyleix, a nice town where he remembered having a drink at a Victorian pub. The taste of Irish whiskey – how could anyone say no to that? But he was going to say no today. He had said no to any whiskey for years now. But the diversion was not for a drink but a trip down memory lane.

'Maybe a cup of tea in the Irish pub!', he told himself remembering a boring story he had read recently. But only when he had finished his tea, he understood that the rich flavour of the Irish tea was clearly one of the best. The day was not going to end with the drive though. It was going to get even busier during the next few days. It was his friend's wedding and that was the reason for his trip to Ireland.

Part II: The wedding

It was a complete surprise when he had got a call about four months back.

'Dave?', asked Andy with his tone clearly registering surprise. It was close to midnight.

'Who did you think was going to wake you up at this time of the night – Scarlett Johansson?', he replied, the usual David Anderson and his sarcasm.

'Fuckin' hell! Dave! How the devil are you?', Andy asked.
'Never been better, mate!', Dave answered.

'You are calling me just to make sure I am not dead, aren't you?', Andy knew there was something Dave wanted to tell him.

'Yes of course! Just to make sure you were alive to be one of my groomsmen!', Dave said.

'Groomsmen? What the heck are you talking about?', Andy was even more surprised.

'Andy, my friend, I am getting hitched!'

'Bloody hell!', Andy shrieked. *'Is that for real?!'*

'As real as it can be!', Dave said.

'Who is the unlucky one?'

'You know who!', Dave answered.

Honestly, Andy did not have a clue who Dave was talking about. It had been a year and a half since they had last spoken. The world around people took just one second to change and eighteen months was a very long time indeed.

'It's that the fat guy Joe, init?', Andy asked. Joe was Dave's bully in school who later became a good friend.

'Come on, stop kidding around, mate', he said. *'Joe is like a brother to me'*

'Then, who is it?', I asked again.

'Have you ever logged into your Facebook account?', he was starting to be annoyed.

'I have a Facebook account?', Andy did not even have a slightest clue.

'Ok, you live in the stone age. The lucky one is... Rochelle', Dave said.

'Rachel?!', Andy asked in a startled tone.

'I know you cannot forget Rachel, my dear friend. But, I said, Rochelle. R.o.c.h.e.l.l.e', Dave stressed.

Life had a weird way of reminding people of those things that they are trying hard to forget. But that's how the bitch called life played her game. It has been a good few years since Rachel had left him. But he still remembered every second of their life together. Just her thoughts were enough to bring a rushing pang of guilt.

'Rochelle – got it', Andy said.

'Yes!', Dave responded with a contagious enthusiasm. He spent a long time talking about Rochelle. The story was quite long, boring and filled with the clichés from about ten different movies. (It was even more boring that this story, trust me!)

'That's what love does to you', Andy finally said though he had not given it a speck of attention.

'So, you ok to be a groomsman?', Dave asked.

At that moment, Andy would have said yes to anything if Dave would let him go to sleep. But he was genuinely happy for Dave and he said, *'Yes, I would be very happy to. You know I would do anything for you, David'*.

'I know', Dave said with a smile before he hung up.

And, there he was in Ireland, after all those years, looking forward to his friend's wedding. He got back on the road after a refreshing break and drove nonstop to Cork. The venue for the wedding was the Charleville Park Hotel. The rooms were booked out for the guests well in advance. His suite was booked for seven straight days.

As he was walking to what was going to be his home for the next few days, Dave called him on his mobile. He was supposed to meet Andy at five. Andy thought the phone call was mostly to inform that he was running late.

'Where the hell are you?' Dave said without even a hello.

'I just reached and I am on my way to my room'

'Get your arse down here right now!', Dave commanded. His enthusiasm was quite up there. The days closer to the wedding did have that effect on most people.

The name of the hall that Dave gave me was in the far end of the hotel. Walking through the endless corridors was *'The Shining'* in itself. As Andy came closer to the hall, he felt the rhythmic beats through the walls of the building. There was an fantastic buzz through the door ahead of him. And the rich smell of Irish whiskey. Andy was hoping Dave was going to show him the wedding arrangements in the hall. But he had just walked into a high voltage party.

Andy had not set foot in a party for very long time. Alcohol had ruined his life once and that was quite enough. Dave was nowhere to be seen.

'How could anyone see in this bizarre blinding lighting?', Andy wondered. But that was entirely a different question. He tried asking a few people for Dave but talking was not a possibility with the music so loud.

'Damn!', Andy thought.

Wading through the sudden rush of people, Andy finally found Dave dancing on the stage that was setup in one end of the hall. He was having a good time. Andy didn't know how Dave found him but he did. He jogged through the crowd and hugged him.

'What took you so long?', he shouted over the music.

Dave had a Van Dyke – a peculiar choice for a wedding, Andy thought. He looked a lot more matured than Andy had last seen him. After all, getting married and starting a new phase of life was going to need a lot of maturity.

The music was getting louder every other minute and talking to each other well, shouting to each other was annoying. And with some weird hand gestures, it was tiring.

Finally, Andy managed to convey, *'I will be in the corner'*.

'But you have not met Rochelle yet!', Dave shouted back. He signaled Andy to wait while we went to find Rochelle.

Andy waited a few minutes and was in no mood to be there. The smell of alcohol – that rich intoxicating smell was playing with his senses. Andy hoped he would resist it.

The lights went out for a few seconds. Whether it was part of the DJ's plan for the next number or just a minor problem, Andy did not know. When the lights came back on, Andy saw Dave walking towards him. He was walking with a beautiful girl in a gracious blue dress.

'Should be Rochelle', Andy thought but he was not able to see her face.

And then she turned to face him. Andy's heart stopped beating.

Her eyes! Those blue eyes! Those beautiful blue eyes.

Andy had trouble breathing.

Those eyes! Calm as the clear blue sky.

Andy's vision started to blur and his knees went weak.

Those eyes! Mysterious as the deep blue sea.

He could not believe what he was seeing. He gasped for breath as if he was thrown into deep dark water.

'Oh God!', he gasped. Dave waved at Andy. But Andy took a step back.

'This can't be true', Andy muttered to himself as he took another step back.

'Holy...'

Dave was telling him something.

'...Mother...'

Dave was still telling him something.

'...of God...!'

Before Andy knew it, he bumped into someone behind him and fell hard on the table crashing it along with a few bottles and more than a few glasses. His head was spinning and it was getting dizzier every second. He was not sure if the fall had anything to do with it but he was very sure that those damned blue eyes had everything to do with it!

Dave came running to make sure he was ok. He knelt down beside Andy and shook him, *'Are you ok, matey?'*

Andy was trying to blurt out something but he was not able to speak. He was trying really hard but to no effect. Just before he blacked out, he pointed to the girl next to Dave and finally said something.

'That... That is my wife. That is Rachel'.

Part III: Rochelle Aibhilin McCarthy

When he woke up and his vision cleared, he was looking into them again - Those blue eyes. Slowly his thoughts came back. The girl's face became clear. Her features were brighter now. She had aged a little – five years was a long time. After what felt like a millennium since she left him, he was face to face again with her. He was looking at Rachel.

The name kept following him ever since she had left him. But he never found her. His searches never led to the real Rachel. He found one Rachel a few years back but it was someone else who he took home to her parents. It was then that Andy had found the spirit to help people. His search for Rachel and his failure at that had made him help others who were like him.

And, when he had lost hope... When he had lost every track leading to her... When memories of her were the only things left... There she was! In the last place he ever expected her to be. There she was hand in hand with his friend.

Life... It was definitely a bitch!

She was the one attending to him to make sure he was ok. She was always the doctor when the world needed. There was a look of concern on her face. There was recognition in her eyes.

'How could she forget me? I am her husband, damn it!', Andy thought. *'True love is forever, isn't it?'.*

She was asking him something but Andy was not paying attention. She snapped her fingers like she always did and asked him to concentrate.

'Look at me. Can you hear me?', she continued. Of course, Andy was looking at her and it was the only thing he was doing.

'Are you able to hear me?', she asked again and Andy nodded. *'Are you ok?*

'I guess', Andy shrugged.

Then her face changed. The concern was no longer there. The recognition in her eyes vanished in a flash. Andy looked at Dave and then at her. Without a hint or hesitation, she slapped Andy hard and square across his face and furiously in a thick Irish accent asked, *'Who the fuck do you think you are?!'*

She pushed Dave who was trying to calm her down and walked out of the party.

'You alright, Andy?', Dave asked and he nodded.

He gestured Andy to stay and ran behind the girl, who in the next few days, was going to marry him.

'Oh crap! What have I done!', Andy was furious with himself. He managed to get back on his feet and waded through the stares of a million eyes into the garden hoping some fresh air would clear his mind. Dave was there having a tough time trying to calm her down.

'Is that the friend whom you always talked about?', she was furious.

'Come on Rochelle – he had just fallen down and crashed a table. He must have a concussion or something!', Dave said.

'Stop defending him, Dave... For God's sake! Do you even know how embarrassing it is?!' she said. *'And why did he call me Rachel?'*

'I am not defending him Rochelle', Dave tried again. *'I am just asking you to calm down!'*

'I am going back to my room. Make sure you keep him away from me. Next time I might end up breaking his nose', she said walking away fast. *'Or even kill him if...'*

'Rachel!', someone said from behind them. It was Andy.

'Not a good time, mate', said Dave visibly annoyed.

'Rachel! Its Andy!', he said again. She turned around and her face was more furious than before.

'How can you not remember me?', he continued.

'David, do me a favour. Do all of us a favour. Please get your friend out of here before it all goes terribly wrong!', she said. *'And I am not Rachel, you son of a....'*

'Rochelle, it is ok', Dave interrupted before Rochelle said anything.

Andy was almost going to crumble to pieces.

'How do you think I would remember you? This is the first bloody time I am seeing you!', Rochelle shouted.

Dave was going to say something before which Andy started speaking with a blank face.

'You are Rachel Jane Cooper. You were born on the fifteenth of June in England. You were adopted and brought up in New Jersey. You love cheese cakes. You love walking along the river by yourself. You are a doctor – an Emergency Physician. You are allergic to cats. You love dogs. You have a Rottweiler named Barney. You are ambidextrous. You love feeding the pigeons. You get dreams about a farm house. You dream about looking at yourself into a bedazzled mirror. You have a birth mark on the right side of your head like a squiggly Z. You get weird pain in your arms and legs for no apparent reasons. You cried yourself to sleep once saying you could not move your leg when we were on the cruise to Santa Monica. You fell down and broke your hand once in..', Andy stopped and stammered for a second to remember when it was.

126

'...in July 2006', Rochelle finished his sentence. Dave and Andy looked at each other and turned towards her in unison.

And then, she fainted.

'Ah man, what is with the fainting, both of you?!', he complained and ran to see if Rochelle was alright.

Dave carried Rochelle to their room. Andy did not know what to do. He had already done enough damage. He had crashed the party, made Rachel or Rochelle whoever it was, furious and Dave - he had not said anything but he would be taking it out on him.

The hotel physician attended to Rochelle. He assured Dave that it was exhaustion and she would be fine after a good sleep. Dave left her at peace and walked to Andy's room with a bottle of Tullamore Dew. Andy had spent almost an hour in the shower letting his emotions flow down with the hot water. When Dave knocked at the door Andy was a little worried. They glanced at each other uneasily

'You are not going to break that bottle on my head, are you?', Andy asked.

Dave looked at the bottle and said, *'That was the plan but I didn't want to waste the whiskey'.*

'I am not furious with you...' he continued. *'...yet'.*

Dave took a gulp a gulp and gave the bottle to Andy who refused it with his usual, *'That's not for me anymore'*

'It did not go quite the way you wanted, did it?' Andy asked.

'Not even a bit', Dave answered and gulped some more of the whiskey.

'We need to talk, Dave', Andy said. *'...in detail'*.

'Absolutely! But not without Rochelle', Dave replied. *'That won't be fair'*.

Andy understood. He had put his friend in a delicate situation and he did not want to make it any worse. They just spent some more time discussing random things till Dave was sloshed and asleep. He somehow woke up when his phone rang well past midnight. It was Rochelle. Dave went back to his room, kissed Rochelle gently and hugged her to sleep.

Andy woke up just after Dave had left and he had trouble sleeping after that. The blue eyes were staring at him every time he closed his eyes. He had messed his life up long back and in a momentary spur of reaction, he had almost messed up his friend's life as well. He had seen Rachel; at least he thought she was, after about five years. He had now created a problem for all the three of them. He had to fix it for everyone's sake. Somehow, he had to!

At about seven in the morning the next day, Andy received a text message from Dave asking him to meet them at a restaurant with a weird name on the Miller Street. They obviously didn't want to talk in the hotel where a lot of other guests for the wedding were staying.

He found a map at the hotel reception and took a walk to the restaurant. It was a pleasant day for a change in Cork. In Scotland they usually said, *'If you hate the weather now, just wait for fifteen minutes'*. The weather changed almost as quickly in Ireland as well. But the weather had been at its best behaviour thus far that morning.

Just outside the restaurant, he saw a homeless man. Andy bought some food for him and sat down next him talking for some time. The man was curious to see someone like Andy but was happy. It was just something that Andy did all the time, it made him happy as well.

When Rochelle and Dave arrived in a cab, Andy and the homeless man were sharing a few laughs. Dave waved Andy to come in to what was going to be the awkward encounter of the year. Almost about the same time, a car arrived in the Charville Park Hotel. A man walked up to the reception and asked for Andrew Reynolds. The other man waiting in the car had a scar on his face and tattoos covered his entire arm.

Just as he was taking his seat, Rochelle asked him suddenly, *'You are not stalking me, are you? How the hell do you know so much about me?'*. Andy and Dave exchanged a glance. They didn't expect the situation to be hostile right away.

Rochelle gave it a second and smiled, *'Relax! I was just messing with you!'*, to the two men's relief.

'Let me be clear about something to both of you', Rochelle began. *'I am not Rachel. Are we clear on that?'*

Dave nodded immediately. Andy did not know how that could be but agreed to start with.

'Rachel...', Andy began.

She stopped him right there. *'Andy, I said you know so much about me but I didn't say each and everything was right. You were close but not each and everything was right'.*

'What do you mean?', Andy asked.

'All right, let me start with the name. I am Rochelle not Rachel. I have been Rochelle McCarthy for all my life – Rochelle Aibhilin McCarthy', she said. Her thick Irish accent was not making it any easier for Andy to follow.

'Rochelle Aibhilin McCarthy?', Andy asked with a smirk.

'Yes. I was born in England – yes. I was adopted – yes. But I did not grow up in New Jersey. I grew up in Dublin. I have never crossed the pacific in my entire life'. It was certainly getting weird.

Andy started to say something again, but Rochelle stopped him.

'I am a doctor - yes. But a neurologist. I love cheesecakes. I love walking along the river by myself - All that is correct. I am allergic to cats. I had a Rottweiler named Barnicle – almost Barney like you mentioned yesterday. Yes, I have recurring dreams. I dream as if I am standing in a balcony watching the sun rise in the east. And yes, I get these weird aches and pains you mention about'

'Ah come on, you even knew the dates', Andy interrupted.

'Yes, in July 2006 I spent two long weeks in pain without the doctors being able to find a single problem with my arm – not

even a sprain', she said. *'So, I didn't break my arm in July 2006. But I broke my leg once...'*

'The awful pain in the leg during the cruise', Andy finished not knowing where this was going.

'Let me ask you something, Andy', she continued. *'Which side of my head did you say I had a birth mark?'*

Andy did not have to think, *'My right, your left. Like a mirrored S - More like a wiggly Z'.*

'Gotcha!' Rochelle snapped with a smile. Dave finally understood something and smiled too.

'Are you sure you are not messing up your right and left hands?' he asked Andy. Andy understood he was missing something that Dave and Rochelle were clear about.

'Rochelle has a big scar on the right side of her head - Her right and your Left'. Dave said making the connection. *'And it looks more like an S'*

'If the connections I am making are right... If I had done my research right twelve years ago...', Rochelle waited for a second controlling her excitement. *'I know who Rachel is!'*

Part IV: The twins

'Your twin sister?!' Andy freaked out. *'It's not some weird joke, is it?'*

'Well, it's not a joke that's for sure. I am just telling you what I think I know', Rochelle said.

*'Well, how do you **think** you know?'*, Andy asked with a straight face.

'It's a long story, Andy', Rochelle said.

'Surprise me!', Andy said leaning back comfortably folding his arms. He clearly was not getting any of it.

Rochelle thought about it for a few seconds and began, *'I don't know my real parents. From what I was told, I was born in London and was given up for adoption when I was six months old.'*

'My parents, John and Daisy who adopted me, took care of me like their own daughter. They added the name Aibhilin to my name because it means "longed-for child." When I was twelve, they sat me down and told me that I was adopted. I was a bright kid and I had figured that out myself when I was about eight. So, it never really bothered me.'

'But there were a lot of things I never understood about me. For example, the bloody big scar on my head. When I was small, believe me, the scar was annoyingly big - Your left... My right...', She said to Andy to make sure he was following.

'You had my curiosity. Now, you have my attention', Andy quoted Tarantino, a touch annoyed with the way it was going.

'And the other things like my mood swings, the weird dreams that were almost real, the excruciating episodes of pain in my arm etc.', she stopped for a second.

'My dreams were mostly of me standing in a balcony looking at the beautiful sunrise', Rochelle said. *'And me feeding*

pigeons – they all had blue rings on their feet as if they were tagged'

'And, you mentioned pigeons yesterday?', Dave asked.

Andy nodded, *'Rachel loved those pigeons. They had to sell them when she was fifteen. They lived in an apartment with a balcony where Rachel said she would stand everyday watching the sunrise',* Andy added.

'I grew up on a farm house outside Dublin', Rochelle said.

'Just like in Rachel's dream', Andy said staring into the void.

'The thing is...', Rochelle continued after a moment's thought.

'Ever since I was a kid, I felt I had two lives - One here in Dublin and another in a place unknown. My instincts, my mind, my body, everything said there was something more to it', the words almost choked in Rochelle's throat.

'I learnt to live with it because no one had any answers. And after all these years you come along out of the blue and confirm what I had thought all my life'.

Andy controlled his thoughts. All the while a small part of him said this was Rachel. But that was not the case.

'I did a lot of research about twins, Andy. All the nature vs nurture studies, the telepathic ability between twins and humpty weird facts about how separated twins think so much alike', Rochelle continued as tears gathered in her eyes.

'All the things we talked about now will make it to the list of "THE MOST AMAZING FACTS ABOUT TWINS". But what people fail to understand is the difficulty each of the separated twin faces. They don't write or care about how a twin like me would miss a part of life - The part that I didn't even have a clue about. They don't know the inexplicable void there is in my mind', Rochelle sobbed.

'Life is a bitch', Andy said. *'...A real bitch'.*

'I did my best to trace my roots. I went to London to try and talk to the people who helped with the adoption and the hospital. The details were sketchy as the hospital records were lost in a fire. All I could find was a record of Craniophagus twins born on the day I was born. I just think I was one of those twins'.

'English please, Doctor?', Dave asked.

'Twins joined at the cranium', she said tapping her head. *'The skull'*

Andy and Dave let the moment settle in waiting for Rochelle to calm down.

'Do you have any dreams of where your sister is now?', Andy asked partly curious, partly selfish.

'Really, Andy? That's your question?' Rochelle was slightly annoyed as well as amused with the question. *'I said I was a twin not a psychic!'*

Dave was the one to giggle first.

'Oh, knock it off Dave!' Rochelle said.

'Come on, the last bit was funny. You've got to give me that!', Dave said.

And then Andy giggled. And slowly Rochelle laughed too. Finally, the situation turned a little less hostile. They laughed at each other making fun of what had happened in the last half a day. As they gulped down their coffees, Dave asked, *'you really love her, don't you Andy? Even after all these years'.*

Andy nodded. He still loved her with all his heart.

He looked at Rochelle. He looked at her blue eyes. He remembered the face of the woman who he loved so much - the face of Rachel. Just as he was about to get lost in his thoughts Rochelle asked him, *'So, what's your story Andy?'*

Silence was Andy's response.

'How did the two of you meet? And, why did she leave you?' she asked again.

'She didn't leave me. I... I pushed her out of my life', Andy said furious with himself.

'But I thought you said you loved her?'

'Yes, I did. I still very much do', Andy's thoughts went back to the day – the time it all happened.

'It's a long story, Rachel', Andy said. *'Sorry! It's a long story, Rochelle'*

'Come on Andy', Dave said. *'Now is best for both of us to know. I never got to hear the full story before'*

That little moment when someone fell in love – it is one of those unexpected and inexplicable things in life. It was the same with Andy too. He remembered that second to the extreme precision. That first little second when their eyes met. That one second that felt like a lifetime. That one second that changed everything.

Part V: Rachel Jane Cooper

It was four minutes to one and he had to run back from his lunch break pretty soon. His daily lunch was a chicken wrap from the old Lebanese cafe. It was the same routine ever since the first day at work. He had taken the bench in the corner of the square staring at the pigeons hopping all around him. They looked radiant as their feathers glittered in the afternoon sun. He sat there just lost in the world of pigeons.

'Beautiful, aren't they?' said someone from behind him. He didn't turn around but nodded looking at the pigeons.

'We had a lot of pigeons at home when I was young', the voice continued.

'That should have been lovely', Andy said still lost in the pigeon world.

And after a minute, he turned around to see who he was talking to. That was when he looked at her for the first time. That's when he saw the beautiful blue eyes. That's when time defied the laws of physics and just decided to hang on to that one second. It was Rachel.

Love sometimes happened just like that, just like a flick of a switch. One second life was normal and a second later, Boom! Love!

All Andy wished at that moment was, *'If the world had to end, let it be now! Let these eyes be the last thing I would ever have to see!'*

But, that was where everything began – just began.

Rachel could not say a word. Actually, she wasn't even breathing. Though it was just a phrase used in a gazillion love stories, Rachel felt it was very real – her heart had just literally skipped a beat.

They just looked at each other oblivious to the world around them. The clock just kept on ticking but neither of them seemed to notice it. Andy's phone rang about four times and Rachel's phone about six times – they just didn't notice.

Not knowing what to do next, Andy lent his hand out to her and...

'You didn't ask her to marry you, did you?', Dave interrupted.

'Shut up, Dave!', Rochelle was filled with curiosity. *'What happened then, Andy?'*

'Most definitely not!', Andy smiled. *'You seem a little bored, mate. Let's get more coffee – what say?*

'Yeah! This seems to be a very long story!', Dave sighed. They got a refill and Andy got back to his story.

Memories Of The Blue Eyes

Andy lent out his hand and introduced himself and so did Rachel. Then they went back to locking eyes. At some point, not knowing how or what to talk about Andy said, *'So... Pigeons?'*

'Yes, Pigeons – I love pigeons!', Rachel almost jumped back on her feet

'And, I love you', Andy blurted. Her eyes went wide with a sparkle. She was either surprised or amused.

'I mean... your eyes. Your eyes are the most beautiful I have ever seen', Andy said.

Rachel blushed as they both stood up and took a step closer to each other. The pigeons swirled around them like a fairy's love spell taking effect on them. That one second felt like a lifetime. That one second changed everything.

Amidst the love and excitement, years flew by before they took notice, they were married and were headed in the *'happily ever after'* fairy tale direction. They had huge plans for their future.

'A daughter like you and a son like me', Andy said one day smiling at Rachel. *'She will have your beautiful eyes! Those blue eyes!'*

'Two sons! Just like you, Andy!', Rachel said. *'They can have my eyes, though!'*

Life indeed was heading in the *'happily ever after'* direction. But as Andy always said, Life was a bitch – Bitch with a capital B. It was 2008 – the year that shattered the lives of so many people including theirs. The financial world collapsed. But the entire world collapsed for Andy and Rachel.

Andy's firm closed down. His savings quickly disappeared and finding a new job was close to impossible. He tried his best to do what he could but depression caught up quickly – quicker than they could even notice.

Rachel was getting more and more depressed as the days went by. She tried as best as a loving wife could. She tried her best to be stable and lift Andy's spirits. And one day Andy came home drunk. That was when she knew he had become impossible. After a few days, it became an addiction. He started coming home in the wee hours completely sloshed.

Rachel tried in vain every single day to talk some sense into him. She cried to him and begged him to amend his ways but it was becoming useless day by day. Andy kept pushing her to her limits till she decided it was enough. It was three in the morning when Andy stumbled into the living room. She kept talking and crying but Andy was too drunk to understand. And when she said *'I will leave you! I will leave you for good!'*, Andy lost it.

He did not mean it and it was more of a spur of the moment kind of reaction. Before he could get a handle on his thoughts, his arm swayed and landed a punch on Rachel's face. And it all ended there. They never spoke a word after that. They never saw each other again.

When Andy woke up the next morning, the house was empty. Rachel had left him a note that she was leaving him. She had said in the note that she still loved him as much as she

Memories Of The Blue Eyes

did the moment they had met but she had realised that Andy had none of it. Just like that, it was all over for Andy.

When people fell out of relationships, it was never the love that died. Love never left them. People did. People died, people walked out. True love just waited for them to realise its existence but people, for one reason or the other, pretended that there was no more love. Andy searched for her for many days. He tried every avenue he could to locate her and travelled to every place they had been together. But she had disappeared from his life without a trace.

Andy could not believe she was not there anymore. Just like that one second they fell in love, he remembered very well, that one second when everything fell apart. He could never forget the first time he saw her eyes – those beautiful blue eyes sparkling with love. He could never forget the last time he saw her eyes – those furious blue eyes filled with rage and tears.

Those eyes haunted him every day, every minute and every second. She had gone away from his life for good but her memories were still fresh like the morning dew. Andy had never ending dreams where he just stared into the abyss of those beautiful eyes.

Weeks became months. Months became years.

Andy could not find Rachel again. Andy reached his final place to search – St Ives, Cornwall. That was the last place of hope for Andy. Rachel had an aunt of sorts there. Andy had hoped that she would have gone there as a place of last resort. But as fate would have it, she had not been there. After St Ives, Andy had no hope of finding her. And along with it, he lost the hope to live. With all the hurt and guilt building up inside him, he decided at that moment that it was enough. It would all end that night.

He had bought himself a bottle of whiskey and walked up to a deserted corner of the Beach Road. He had decided to gulp down the whiskey one last time and drown in the sea. End it once and for all.

Just as he opened the bottle, he heard a group partying at a fair distance from him. They all seemed pretty drunk. And before anyone could realise what was happening, there was a loud splash into the sea. Andy realised something was very wrong. Someone had fallen into the water and none of the others were sober enough to realise the seriousness. At that moment Andy forgot what he was doing and ran to help. Without a moment's hesitation, he jumped into the water to save a life.

The man he saved that night turned out to be Dave. He was drunk and disoriented after the moment but he knew Andy had saved his life. But Andy felt the other way round - David had saved his. When Andy and Dave met a few days later, they became good friends and, though they did not say it, owed each other their lives.

'You guys have been friends for years but how come you didn't know how Rachel looked?', Rochelle asked Dave.

'We have spoken for hours together about my search for Rachel and I remember showing Dave her picture a couple of times. But, the only rational explanation I can think of is that he has a memory as bad as a Chimp'.

That brought about a much-needed laughter in the group. Having caused a stir the previous day, Andy felt a little less guilty after that morning. Each one of the three needed to really know what was going on.

'Promise me one thing, Andy', Rochelle said as they stepped out of the restaurant. *'Promise me you will find Rachel one day!'*

Andy smiled and thought about it for a second. *'That is what I hope for every single day'*

Before they started walking he said, *'I promise I will find her'*

When they got out onto the high street it was pretty deserted given it was the middle of the day. There was just one car in the vicinity and it was coming towards them. Little did they know that the men in that very car had been looking for Andy the whole morning.

Part VI: When his heart skipped a beat

Just as the car crossed them, it came to screeching stop. Three men rushed out of the car and one of them had a huge scar on his face. He was the drug lord who had his gun on Andy's head a few weeks back. Andy felt the blood drain off his face. He knew something very bad was going to happen.

The man broke into a strange smile showing the drug stained teeth all at once – a smile that would send a shiver down the spine of them all. When the gun came out of his coat pocket, Andy's world went quiet. Andy couldn't hear a thing. He could not hear Rochelle and Dave scream, he could not hear the gunshot, and he could not hear the shop window shatter. It was as if he was in a vacuum chamber. He did not feel a thing as he collapsed to the ground. As his vision blurred, he saw Rochelle run to him and before he closed his eyes, he heard a distant sound of a siren and the last things he saw were Rochelle and her beautiful blue eyes.

Up until that point it was just another ordinary day in the Mercy Hospital in Cork. It all changed when the speeding ambulance rushed in. Andy was covered in blood but was, with considerable difficulty, still breathing. He had three bullet wounds and had lost a lot of blood. He was in and out of consciousness for a good few minutes.

'Don't you fucking die, you son of a bitch!', Dave kept shouting into Andy's ears. Andy's vision was so blurred that he could not see anything.

'You will be fine! You will be fine!', Rochelle kept saying into his ears with the composure of a doctor that she was.

Andy's world went quiet again. He could not hear anything except for his breath. And once in a while he felt his heartbeat sending a shudder through his head. He was not scared of the severe stillness that the world around him had come to. His eyes fought with all the willpower to stay open. His eyes kept searching those beautiful blue eyes one last time.

And then... *he flatlined.*

'Flat line! Flat line!', the ER nurse shouted to the ER physician who came running. The ER physician stopped when she saw Rochelle and both of them froze. Both of them turned pale like they had seen a ghost. Unable to wait even a second

longer the physician ran into the Emergency Room with her heart pounding.

'What's it, Rochelle?', Dave asked. But she could barely utter a sound. There were too many things happening around them that it was overly exhausting. She just stood there frozen for a good few minutes.

Just as the physician reached Andy, her hands started trembling. She knew who he was. The assistant had just tried to resuscitate him but the CPR was a failure. Still in shock, she motioned for the defibrillator.

'CLEAR!', they attempted to revive his heart. Andy's body jolted. But, nothing.

She signaled for a change in voltage and screamed *'Again!'*

'CLEAR!', they tried again. Still nothing.

'Again!', she shouted with tears rolling down her eyes.

Nothing. *'He's gone, Doc!'*, said one of the assistants not knowing what to do.

'Oh God, no!', she gasped as her knees lost strength and tears started rolling down her eyes in a hurry. None of the people there understood her emotional response to the situation.

'No! Not like this!', she kept saying shaking her head.

'Not like this!', she said again.

Just as she placed her hands on his chest looking at him closely, there was a beep. There was just a tiny little spike on the electrocardiogram as if his heart had skipped a beat. And when she touched his hand, he took a deep breath and his heart started beating again. With the severe pain rushing through his body and fighting all the drugs he had been given, Andy opened his eyes. His eyes locked with those beautiful blue eyes.

Those beautiful blue eyes – calm as the clear blue sky.

Those beautiful blue eyes – mysterious as the deep blue sea.

The name on the doctor's badge said *Jane*. It was *Rachel Jane Cooper*.

Something had to be done...

I don't recognize the man sitting in front of me anymore. His blue eyes are filled with tears. They look tired and without life. He doesn't, in any way, look the way I have known him all the years. We have been looking at each other for quite a while now. He looks like he has woken up from a bad dream. He has not spoken a word since I sat down in front of him and neither have I. There is no tension in the air. There is no love in the way we looked at each other, either. There is just a weird plain blankness between us.

He gave me the news yesterday morning that our marriage was not working out. He wanted to leave me. Just like that. He was going to leave me.

Just like that.

People call me Mrs. Sanderson. I hate that name. My name is Michelle Sanderson but my husband insisted everyone called me Mrs. Sanderson. I didn't mind after a while.

Every single person who knew us thought we were the happiest and the most perfect couple they had ever seen. That might have been true given that we were happy when we were with others. I looked happy and he looked even happier. But that was all for the show. I have no idea why I played along for that long – quite long. Behind the heavy makeup and a beautiful looking life were a million things others did not know about.

So, we are married for two years eleven months and eight days as of today. And add three years four months and one day to that for being together. Things looked all rosy and shiny before we got married. I was genuinely happy every minute I was with him. I have no regrets of those times. He made me laugh, he made me cry with happiness. It was all working like a fairy tale.

When he went down on his knees at a ball game in front of a million people and asked me if I would marry him, I was jubilant and over the moon. Of course, I said yes – who wouldn't. He was the kind of man that every woman would fall head over heels for.

The wedding was grand and beautiful. I still remember the vows – word for word. I remember everything that happened on my wedding day – minute by minute. It was the most colourful and beautiful wedding I had seen in my life. It was, like everyone else who gets married, the most memorable day of my life.

But the reason that stands out to make that day etched in my memory is... It was the last day I was happy. And it's been two years eleven months and eight days since I had a genuine smile on my lips. This was not because of the usual reasons where people just argue their marriage to an end. This was not because of all the usual *men are from Mars* and *women are from Venus* kind of crap that brings a marriage crashing to its knees. It was all due to a painful and immensely powerful reason.

He is a sadist. Yes, you heard that right. My husband is a fucking sadist.

How I did not have even the slightest of clues about this in the entire three years of my life with him before that still remains a mystery to me. May be as they say, Love is blind. Or maybe it was me who was fucking blind all along. But that was it. My life just fell into an abyss even before I realised where it was heading. One day it was all sunshine and then the setting sun never came up again in my life.

I remember the first day the nightmares began. He held my hands in his. What I thought was a romantic was the painful beginning to all the worse things that were in store. He just kept squeezing my hand till I screamed in pain and the skin turned completely purple for the lack of blood. When I fell on the floor almost faint with pain, he smiled at me. I remember that shiver it sent down my spine. I still remember that fucking smile. The nightmare was just beginning.

The endless hours of torture cannot even be explained in words. The punches, kicks, the cigarette burns, you name it. I have gone through them all. The documented cliches, yes. But true – every single word. He smiled through my suffering. He found happiness in every scar he gave me. He found satisfaction in every drop of tear I shed asking him to stop.

And not to mention the rapes. The term marital rape has a weird definition in a everyone's minds. I can't even understand how in some countries marital rape is not even considered a crime against women – absolute fucking nonsense. The trauma of those days will not leave me any day soon. I might have to live my whole life waking up in the middle of the night screaming for help. I might even have to stay awake my entire life to escape those horrible dreams. There should not be even an argument about what punishments rapists should get. After all, what they do is leave the victim alive but kill everything else in her.

He would, once in a while, pay heed to my words and let me be. But those days were too far and apart that I don't even remember them.

I still try to figure out why I endured all this without doing anything about it. Sometimes he would fall to his knees and cry. He would inconsolably cry screaming that his mind was sick and he could never be normal again. Those moments I felt sorry for him – naïve as a kid. I thought this was like a huge container of bad thoughts in his mind that would at one point he would run out of bad stuff and be a normal person again – even kids nowadays are not that naïve.

I wonder if it was the love I had for him was making my mind quarantine this as just a discomfort. What do they call it with the abuse victims? Well, I think it's called repressed memories. Maybe it's called something else, I don't know. When I think of it now, it just makes me want to throw up. But it was not just one day or one week or a bloody month. Almost three fucking years! I did nothing. I just went through it in the name of love.

It all ended yesterday morning. He looked at me with a smile in the morning. I smiled back for a second but then I felt the chills. I was scared. I was waiting for a painful blow or something. But he calmly said those words that a tiny part of my mind was waiting since the day it all began.

"I am leaving you. I don't think it's working out"

My heart and mind did not have a reaction. There was just some sort of numbness. It did not make me happy. It did not make sad. An inexplicable numbness. But that was not it, oh no! That was just the beginning of it.

I laid my head down on the pillow for a few minutes to let my mind start working again. And when it did, something in me told me to help him leave. *'The earlier he left my life the better it would be for both of us'* said a voice in my mind with a clarity I had not had in a long time.

I started packing his things aside, one little thing at a time. That was when I stumbled upon his journals. It was a complete surprise as I did not know he wrote any journals. I had no right to be surprised given he had been a bad surprise in every way over the entirety of our married life. But the journals piqued my interest when I saw the names given to them. One of them said *'**Michelle**'*.

My hands were shivering when I opened the one with my name on it. In it were all the things that he had done to me written down in excruciating detail. It was a complete record of all the atrocities I had gone through without a sense of remorse but with a sadistic sense of achievement. The numbness in my mind returned but this time, what I read made me throw up.

The other journals were similar. Just that they were not about me, but about other women. There were other women he had done this to. There was a pattern. He was not a sadist. Oh, that seemed to be a simple term. My husband was a fucking psycho. He had harmed women before. He is hurting me now. And I could just feel that the he will not stop. He will harm more women. I just knew it. He sure will. He had just gone from one place to another to unleash hell on a woman's life and then moved on as if it was nothing.

Something had to be done.

Something certainly had to be done.

I look at him now sitting in front of him. He is in no way the man I loved. He does not deserve me in any way. For all I had gone through just in the hope that one day I will have a happy fulfilling life with him, something had to be done.

His eyes are filled with tears. He seems very very tired. The casually sadistic person who had always been energetic, the person who always had the time to torture me, sits in front of me without any energy. He can hardly keep his head up.

I know the reason for it, though. It should be the surge of electric current that ran through his body. Oh yeah, I tased him. Didn't I say something had to be done?

I thought it was a momentary thought that had occurred to me. But the thought lingered on and on and on. And at one point my path ahead was all clear and I had made a clear decision in my mind. I could have just packed his stuff and watched him leave my life. But I had read his journals. If I had to just leave, he would just do the same to someone else.

Something certainly, certainly, had to be done.

It was really a very simple exercise. A... very... simple... exercise. I packed my stuff, booked a ticket to one of those little countries that no one knew existed where I could just disappear without an identity. That was bloody cheap. I bought a taser which, citing self-defense as a reason, was not a big deal.

I waited in the dark corner of the garage for his car to come in. As he stepped out of the car, I tased him – nice and strong. After all the years of seeing him smile every time he burnt a cigarette on my skin, this was an exhilarating experience seeing him convulse and helplessly lose consciousness.

I just strapped him to the passenger seat where he seemed to be deep asleep and drove him all the way to this cabin he owned in the woods. The times we were here, we had not seen another human being for miles and miles. I don't think anyone even knew this place existed. Funny thing – this was where it all got serious in our relationship. We made love for the first time in this secluded cabin. An apt place to end it all, I think.

I look at him now, he is unable to move his arms and legs. They are strapped to the strong dining chair as I sit looking at him from the couch directly opposite to him. He has not said a word because I have gagged him with just enough room for him to keep breathing. Tears flow from his eyes. My heart crumbles to pieces when I see him cry.

I laugh at the fact that I still have feelings for this psycho.

Weird, just plain weird, how a woman's mind works.

Fear fills his eyes. He would have had a big wide smile on his face if our roles were reversed. He would have had a big satisfied smile – this sadistic motherfucker.

I decide it is time. I take the nice sharp knife from the bag. I look at his blue eyes one last time and as if I had done it a million times before, I shrugged and said, **'Sorry dear, something had to be done'**.

And I plunge the knife neatly but firmly into his chest. It is surprisingly easy how smoothly the knife slides into him. There is a lot struggle for a good few minutes and a lot of blood. I cannot look or listen to any of it.

I calm myself down and as I step out of the cabin, a complete silence envelopes me.

Peace.

Peace, at last.

The name is...

'I never really liked your name' the Turk said in his coarse and heavily accented voice.

'And, who the fuck names their son Lucifer?' he smirked.

The barrel of the gun was not new to Lucifer. He had for many times been at both the right and wrong ends of it. But this time, the fear was real. It was very real. He was sure the trigger was going to be pulled and it was all going to go up in flames.

His mother had said in her death bed *'I can see almost every second of my life flash in front of my eyes'*. May be that was what he was going to experience now – every second of his life flashing before his eyes.

Ereyesterday – 04/06/06

'What the fuck is that?' she asked in a tired, bewildered but at the same time very sexy voice.

'What are you talking about?' Lucas asked as he put his trousers on walking away from the bed.

He hated his real name – Lucifer. He had gone by the name Lucas for a very long time. He did not even like to remember his real name after all the taunts he had to go through in his catholic upbringing.

'Who the hell names their son Lucifer?!' he had argued with his mother many times during his teenage years. She had just smiled and never gave him an explanation.

Rebekah held onto to the sheets to cover her beautiful body while she traced her fingers over the scar on his back. She had known him for years and she was sure she had not seen it as it was right below his broad shoulders. A sharp burning sensation rushed through the scar the moment she mentioned it. That caught Lucas by surprise. This was the first sense of pain he could remember in very long time, may be first time ever.

He held his breath to get through the pain. Thirty-three years old and he had never once fallen sick or been to a doctor. Even in all the fights he had been through and through all the cuts and scars all over the body, he never remembered to be in pain.

'You able to see that?' he asked in a tone that registered surprise given his entire body was covered in tattoos and other scars.

'Of course, I can see it' Rebekah said. *'Are you sure it's not something you have contracted? You know, the women, needles, etc etc?'*

'I am sure it's nothing' he said in a dull and tired voice as he slid again into bed with her.

'You smell lovely' he tried to change the subject but before he could start a conversation, she was asleep.

Rebekah owned a strip club that operated well and beyond its means. He worked as a bouncer and security. She technically was just the manager but being the Turk's girlfriend gave her the powers that she could use irresponsibly. The Turk, real name known only to a few, was not on any official records in the country. He was mentioned only in hushed tones. Drugs, women, trafficking, weapons, he had his dirty hands in too many pies.

Lucas had no idea how he was still alive for sleeping with the Turk's girl. If they were caught, he knew his head would be the last of a long list of things to be chopped off his body. The first time it happened, it was more of an accident in one of the corner VIP rooms in the club - in one of the security blind spots. She came onto him and being the devil she was, he was not able to resist. That was just the beginning of the story. Five months on, it was still going on under the covers.

Lucas tried to get back to sleep but his mind kept playing tricks on him. He hardly remembered his uneventful life as a child. The first twelve years were almost blank. He felt as though those years did not exist – no birthdays, no falls from the bicycle, no bullying at school. Nothing came to mind when he tried to think about it.

The time after those lost twelve years were filled with everything that would be hated by every normal human being. Drugs, women, street fights, guns, knives, pimps, strippers and more importantly, blood. That, and lots and lots of anything and everything that would not happen in broad daylight. He had no idea why his thoughts kept wandering but he just realised that he was no different from the Turk. He had done it all.

'Maybe, I have lived my name' he thought.

When he woke up, Rebekah was already dressing up to leave. All he could see was her silhouette – she was a beauty.

'I better leave now and get home before he notices I ain't home' she said and walked without a glance.

'He would cut us into little pieces, burn us and wash away the ashes', Lucas thought to himself. As he tried to sleep for a bit more time, his mind kept delving into the dark corners of his mind that he did not know existed. The new scar on the back was burning more than it did before.

Yesterday – 05/06/06

The dreams kept coming back to him all day. When he finally woke up by midafternoon, something in him seemed completely changed. He could not think straight. The memories were far and apart but there was an overwhelming sense of power in his mind and body when he walked out of his house.

His mind was buzzing with dark thoughts as he took his spot just near the entrance of the club. There were not many customers though it was half price for all lap dances and anything else the women were willing to do. Rebekah was nowhere to be seen which he thought was good given the state he was in. After about thirty minutes of no activity, his eyes began to roll. He could sense there was something bad approaching. He could not think of what that would be. To break the monotony of the evening, a car slowly came into view. He had seen the car a lot of times before and knew who it was.

'Massimo', Lucas nodded as the man entered the club. He had known Massimo for quite a long time. He was the spoilt kid brother of the Turk. He was the Turk in the making, only a far smaller brain. Massimo was more brawn but effective nevertheless. But Lucas knew Massimo spelt trouble everywhere he went, especially at the club. The women hated him, the bouncers hated him and more importantly Rebekah

hated him. But being the Turk's brother got him into anything and everything he wanted.

Lucas felt more and more uncomfortable as time went by. There was some kind of metamorphosis he was going through. Something was changing in him and somehow, he knew there was nothing good about it.

'You look pale, man' said another bouncer. *'Your eyes look cold and blue!'*

This surprised Lucas as his eyes were green as far as he could remember. But before he could say anything, there was a commotion in the club. It was Massimo causing trouble as usual. He and the latest addition to the payroll were not getting along well. He had created a big scene and the stripper ended up with a broken nose. Everyone had left their stall and had gathered around Massimo. When Lucas reached, Rebekah was asking him to leave.

'Fuck you, bitch!' he said right to her face. But Rebekah was made of steel – enough to run a club like that. Lucas tried to calm Massimo down but he was not paying heed. He had to be literally dragged away to the parking lot.

'Who do you think you are?!' screamed Massimo as he spit on Lucas' face. *'You think you can get away with me?!'* he laughed. Rebekah was out with them to get Massimo back in his car and be done for the night but it was all getting out of hand.

Massimo stared long and hard at Lucas and screamed *'Do you think sleeping with this bitch makes you think you are bigger than me?'*

Whether it was the deluded state he was in or the growing sense of power in him, Lucas lost it that second and landed a strong jab behind Massimo's ear.

Everything went quiet after that.

Massimo's eyes blinked a few times and then blood flowed from his nose and ear. A deafening silence enveloped Lucas. It was not just the silence. He could see people talking to him and people screaming but nothing registered in his mind.

He just saw Massimo's lifeless body dead on the dirty road. He did not really understand what he had done. He was in a state of complete trance. But he knew he was in a deadly mess. He had to get away from the place. He did not care who was screaming. He did not care who was dead. He did not care what Rebekah was saying. He didn't even give a shit that he had killed someone.

'I have to disappear', was all his thoughts.

As he got into Massimo's car, he heard shots fired. A quick look over the shoulder confirmed he was the target.

He felt a surge of pain in his back just below the shoulder. He did not know if he was shot but the pain was unbearable and still surging. He screamed as he put the metal to the floor and the car jumped with a roar. The pain was immense. He felt something clawing its way through the nerves and muscles all over his body. He did not know if he was bleeding but the surge of adrenaline kept him going.

He always had plans for contingencies like these. Not just now, he always did. Given everything sinister he was involved in, he needed the escape plans. He reached the worn-down storage facility on the outskirts of the city. He picked up the things he required, cash from his emergency reserve, the weapons and ammunition and all the other stuff he thought he would need to stay alive. Suddenly there was a weird clarity in his mind and he felt very alive. He took a deep breath to think clearly.

'Did I really kill him?' he asked himself again and again.

The dreams and hallucinations were never ending. The minute he had stepped out of his house that morning, the day had just gotten worse. He didn't remember anything all through his drive to the personal safe house which only he knew existed. It was an underground cellar in an abandoned warehouse. He could use the time to gather his wavering thoughts and get a plan in place to pull himself out of the grave he found himself in.

Men were going to be looking for him. The Turk was not someone who would not make a mess of him. A bounty would have already been put on his head. And it was most likely forty-eight hours before they came bursting through the door. He had disposed of Massimo's car in the swamp far away from the hideout, dropped his phone even before that. He did not leave a paper trail, no credit cards, no phone calls. He did his best to drop out of the search.

Minutes became hours and he was just in the same seat looking at the door. Whether he was half asleep or if he was dreaming, he did not know. He was back in a trance. His mind was playing with him. He could feel an immense strength inside him that kept growing exponentially. He was, for some reason, evolving continuously.

Too many things and too much shock for the body and mind to handle, he thought to himself. The burning pain on his back had numbed down, thanks to the huge gulps of whiskey. He had taken a look in the mirror. He could only thank his lucky stars that there were no bullet wounds. He was unharmed so far. The only thing, other than being killed by the Turk, was the scar on his back had grown bigger and in every sense weirder. Everything about him and around him was getting more and more scarier.

It was all eerily quiet. He had not stepped out of his safe house for over thirteen hours. He had used a bit of his contacts to get what the Turk was up to. Whatever information he had gathered from the limited resources and contacts he had, the army of the Turk's thugs were looking for him in an entirely different direction.

Lucas settled into the quietness. An enormous feeling of rage, power, strange and bad things were building up in him. He felt a raging animal awakening in him. He gripped the rails on the little bed and waited in silence for his heart to stop racing and his mind to calm down. It was all in vain. The pressure in his head was immense. For a moment, he thought, he would grow wings all of a sudden and burst out of the cocoon. The scar was still growing.

Today 06/06/06 - 05:06 AM

None of the motion sensors had picked up any movement. None of the alarms went off. He was in a quasi-stable state and none of the sounds woke him up completely.

Memories Of The Blue Eyes

A huge blast ripped through the door taking half the wall along with it. Smoke and debris filled the room. The blast threw Lucas against the wall of the room. He was hurt badly on the back and was only barely conscious. He was bleeding from the shrapnel wounds. He could barely sit up. A group of heavy set men walked in and stood in line covering the gaping hole that the blast had left.

'You didn't really think you are safe in this shit hole, did you?'

Lucas could not see who the people were. The coarse voice that said those words was very familiar. It was the Turk. He could see about eight men in the room. He was sure his end was near. And there was someone on their knees with a face hanging with almost no life. Blood was dripping from the face. It took a long time before he realised who that was. It was Rebekah.

It was all coming to an end very soon, he could feel it.

When one of them landed the first punch on the side of his face, he heard his own bones crunch and his teeth give way to accommodate the force. He fell face first on the floor. A kick on the side of ribs made sure he stayed in place. For the first time in a long time, he felt pain - a blinding pain. It was not from the broken bones or the injuries. The blinding pain was from the scar as if there was an animal trying to rip the flesh off.

His eyes met Rebekah's. He did not see fear in her eyes, a woman of steel. She was going to be killed as well, bludgeoned to death in front of his eyes. The Turk was a psycho even before anyone made him mad. But now he was angry, mad and everything else put together. Even the devil himself would think twice before getting into a brawl with that man.

Today 06/06/06 - 05:56 AM

They tied Lucas and Rebekah to the chairs facing each other. Both of them were alive - just about. Everything that was done to them was done to hurt - hurt like death itself. The Turk looked into his eyes with a dead and cold stare. *'Oh don't worry. I won't kill you or your bitch. But...'* he let out a sigh.

'.... you will beg me to!', he stood up crushing Lucas' feet under his thick boot.

The pain inflicted never seemed to be enough. Rebekah's face was unrecognisable. Every inch of her face was bleeding and broken beyond recognition. But her cold blue eyes looked at him with a nerve wrecking resolve. Somewhere in that look of hers, she asked him to put her out of her misery.

The Turk came back into the room pulling a barrel behind him. He emptied most of it on Rebekah. She shivered in pain as the fuel hurt her open wounds. Never once did she scream. Lucas had never seen anyone face fear like she did. The flick of the match sent a shudder down his heart. He knew what was coming.

'No, don't!' he managed to say. *'It was all my fault. Let her go!'* most of his words were just about understandable.

'Don't, what?' the Turk asked with a smile on his face. The match burnt slowly.

'Don't what, Lucas?' his smile turned into a mad laughter.

'Let her live! Kill me!', Lucas said again and again.

'Oh, you don't want me to do this?' the Turk raised his eyebrows as he threw the match stick with a tiny bit of dying flame clinging on to the edge of the stick. The flame caught up quickly. She was engulfed in it before anyone could even blink an eye. The flame would have looked beautiful with its wings waving over and over. But there was nothing but stillness in that broken room.

She did not even wince when the flame burnt through her skin and flesh. She never even let out a breath till her life oozed out of her. She sat still like the burning Tibetan monk. Her blue eyes kept looking at him till the last drop of life evaporated out of her.

Today 06/06/06 - 06:06 AM

The Turk pointed the gun at Lucas. After all he had gone through, Lucas knew the end was near.

'I never really liked your real name' the Turk said in his coarse and heavily accented voice.

'And, who the fuck names their son Lucifer?' he smirked.

The barrel of the gun was not new to Lucifer. He had for many times been at both the right and wrong ends of it. But this time, the fear was real. It was very real. He was sure the trigger was going to be pulled and it was all going to go up in flames.

His mother had said in her death bed *'I can see almost every second of my life flash in front of my eyes'*. May be that was what he was going to experience now – every second of his life flashing before his eyes.

He was not bothered anymore. Not even the gun pointed at him. He was only a pull of the trigger away from an inevitable death. The burning pain from the scar had his attention. The second when Rebekah's life left her body, he felt suddenly the unrecognizable forces pulling his thoughts and gnawing away his brain like rodents. The scar was burning more and more.

Then, all of a sudden, his dizzy vision became very clear. The hands in the Turk's watch had just moved to 06:06:06. Everything he saw around him; the men, the Turk, Rebekah and the burning flames that engulfed her, stood still. Everything just stood still. Time stood still. There was no pain anymore. There was a moment of pure clarity. Everything stood still for him. Everything stood still for Lucifer.

What he could not see was that at about the same time, the scar on the back had morphed into something sinister. It had grown into something that would be recognized by the unknown cults around the world. It had evolved into something the devil himself would wear on him.

He could hear his heart beating slowly, very slowly. No one even blinked their eyes. He looked at his hand, they were not tied anymore. The skin was paler than white. It was ghostly white.

'Maybe, I am dead', he thought. The Turk's finger was still on the trigger. He was yet to pull it. The blood all over his body slowly began to disappear. The cuts and bruises evaporated in

front of his eyes. The sense of power and strength took him by surprise. He felt he had the strength to crush anyone's skull with his hands. The power inside of him was immense and he felt he was about to burst into flames.

And then, when he was ready, time unfroze.

The flame on Rebekah's body danced like it did before. The Turk's eye moved and he pulled the trigger saying the words *'You never had it in you to be named Lucifer. You will always be Lucas!'*.

Lucas watched the trigger engage and the barrel of the gun recoil to spit out the brass bullet at an incredible speed. He saw the spark and the bullet travel towards him slowly and steadily. He could have even caught it on its way towards him with his fingers. But the bullet looked beautiful as it travelled towards him - so beautiful that he let it be.

He felt no pain when the bullet touched his forehead, pierced through his skull and blasted its way on the other side. There was no pain. There was no blood.

The Turk thought he had missed his aim. He shot again and again till he emptied the entire cartridge into Lucas. But nothing happened to him. The scar on his back was glowing like fire. It created a ghastly glow enveloping him. There was nothing beautiful about the way he looked at that moment. The moment sent an inexplicable surge of fear running through everyone.

Lucas smiled. He understood the power in him. It was all clear to him now. He did not look like the person they had seen or known before. He did not look like anything they had seen before.

Lucas stood up and looked at everyone in the room. Their souls left their bodies as he looked into everyone's eyes. They dropped dead one by one like a swarm of flies. He had the power to do anything he wanted.

The Turk could not comprehend what was happening around him. He had no one to back him up. He stood shivering and looked at the man he had come to kill. But who or what stood before him, he did not want to know.

'No Lucas, please don't!', he muttered as the gaze fell on him.

Lucas smiled. Not knowing what to do the Turk smiled too. And the smile on Lucas' face disappeared as quickly as it appeared. The evil power in him surfaced without a hint.

'The Name Is LUCIFER...!!!', he screamed. He screamed so loud that the force pushed the Turk a good few feet into the air.

He went closer to the Turk and whispered into his ears *'It's not just my name!'*

'I...'

'...AM...'

'...LUCIFER...!!!', he screamed.

Then like a wand, he pointed his finger at the big man who was trying to stand up. A quick flame burst out of thin air engulfing the Turk.

As the flame took away all the remaining life in that room, Lucifer took a deep breath and walked out into the world to mark the beginning of its end.

Memories Of The Blue Eyes

Acknowledgements

A huge thank you to my wife Jovie and son Ethan for putting up with my never-ending quest to accomplish a million things at the same time. The time, space and energy they have given me all through is astounding. Jovie – you are my rock. I am eternally grateful to my parents to have given me a rare kind of freedom that not all Indian kids are blessed with – I am what I am because of it. I thank my family and friends who till date are the most difficult critics to convince – how many stories I write and however bad I write, I am sure they will be there to make them a touch better (and of course give me a hard time for it first). I love it when most of them find it difficult to read the stories objectively keeping me out of their mind. I love it even more when they say the words 'You have changed!'. I find that a big victory as a storyteller that I have given them something unexpected. Special thanks to two of my friends: Firstly, Anandraj Thiyagarajaperumal who has been one of the few people who have been patient with my decades of jibber-jabber. That all-nighter he pulled to give me his feedback was amazing. And Louise Ogle for having spent the time to go through the book word by word to get hundreds of little things right which, in a million years, I would not have noticed. Last but by no means least, a mighty thank you for all those who have come this far to read the book – without the readers, a book does not serve its true purpose.

About the Author

"Everyone has more than a few stories to tell", Peter always says. He prefers to be called a storyteller than a writer. *"Even my conversations have little stories and I write like I talk! For those who know me, that means my writing cannot be great!"*, he usually laughs. Taking inspirations from experiences in life, he has seventeen short stories to his name and aims at substantially increasing that number in the coming years. Born and brought up in India, he now lives with his wife and son in the UK. He is an IT Professional with quite a wide range of hobbies including photography, fitness and a never-ending love for great cinema.

Made in the USA
Coppell, TX
29 January 2021